Dear Readers,

Since I am a fervent  s, I really appreciate ls from other authors ly held together with tape and staples! (This is especially true of my prized Betty Neels Mills and Boon® Romance novels!) So it is a double pleasure for me to be one of the authors chosen for a lovely Collector's Edition from Silhouette Books.

These are some of my favourite titles. I hope you will enjoy these early books of mine, too, some of which were out of print and have been difficult to find. This new edition will make it easier for my readers, to find the scarce books that you may have wanted to add to your collections. And if any of your books are being held together by tape and staples, too, these attractive Collector's Edition volumes will find a niche in your bookcase—just as they have in mine.

Thank you for your kindness, and your loyalty, for so many years.

Your friend and fellow collector,

Diana Palmer

Diana Palmer

DIANA PALMER COLLECTOR'S EDITION

Silhouette Books are proud to present a selection of favourite titles from one of the world's most popular romance writers. They have been brought together to form a very special Collector's Edition for you to cherish and keep.

DIANA PALMER

RAWHIDE AND LACE

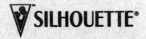

SILHOUETTE®

*Silhouette, and Colophon are
registered trademarks of Harlequin Books S.A.,
used under licence.*

*First published in Great Britain 1987
Silhouette Books, Eton House, 18-24 Paradise Road,
Richmond, Surrey TW9 1SR*

© Diana Palmer 1986

ISBN 0 373 59901 3

79-9809

*Printed and bound in Great Britain
by Caledonian International Book Manufacturing Ltd, Glasgow*

DIANA PALMER

Born and raised in Georgia, Diana Palmer still lives there, in the mountains, with her husband James and their son, Blayne Edward. She began her writing career as a newspaper reporter and certainly has no problems with writer's block. Diana manages on average to write a book every two months!

Diana Palmer wrote her first book for Silhouette® in 1980 and has never looked back since. She now has had more than fifty novels published by Silhouette, as well as historical romances and longer contemporary works by other publishers. Diana is deemed one of the top ten romance writers in America and has more than 32 million copies of her books in print!

Always on the watch for new experiences, Diana recently added a degree in history to her list of achievements. Before that, between novels, she studied the piano, planted flowers, and dreamt of becoming an operative for the CIA. She considers her greatest blessing to be the friendship of her readers.

One
___

The hospital emergency room was full of people, but the tall man never saw the crying children and listless adults who covered the waiting area. He was disheveled, because he'd dragged on jeans and the first shirt that had come to hand and hadn't taken time to shave or even comb his thick, straight black hair.

He stopped at the clerk's desk, his expression enough to get her immediate attention. He looked rough and not in the mood for red tape—his face cold and hard, and very nearly homely.

"Yes, sir?" she asked politely.

"The sheriff's office said my brother was brought here. His name is Bruce Wade," he said, with barely controlled impatience, his voice deep and cutting, his silver eyes piercing and level.

"He was taken to surgery," the clerk said after a minute. "Dr. Lawson admitted him. Just a moment, please."

She picked up the phone, pressed a button and mumbled something.

Tyson Wade paced the small corridor restlessly, his shepherd's coat making him look even taller than he was, the creamy softness of his Stetson a direct contrast to a face that looked like leather and sharp rock. Things had been so normal just minutes before. He'd been working on the books, thinking about selling off some culls from among his purebred Santa Gertrudis breeding herd, when the phone had rung. And all of a sudden, his life had changed. Bruce had to be all right. Ty had waited too long to make peace with the younger brother he hardly knew, but surely there was still time. There had to be time!

A green-uniformed man walked into the waiting area, removing his mask and cap as he walked toward the taller man.

"Mr. Wade?" he asked politely.

Ty moved forward quickly. "How's my brother?" he asked brusquely.

The doctor started to speak. Then he turned, drawing Ty down the white corridor and into a small unoccupied examination room.

"I'm sorry," the doctor said then, gently. "There was too much internal damage. We lost him."

Ty didn't flinch. He'd had years of practice at hiding pain, at keeping his deeper feelings under control. A man who looked like he did couldn't afford the luxury of letting them show. He just stood there, unmoving, studying the doctor's round face while he tried to cope with the knowledge that he'd never see his brother again; that he was totally alone now. He had no one. "Was it quick?" he asked finally.

The doctor nodded. "He was unconscious when he was admitted. He never came out of it."

"There was another car involved," Ty said, almost as an afterthought. "Was anyone else badly hurt?"

Dr. Lawson smiled with faint irony. "No. The other car was one of those old gas-guzzlers. It was hardly dented. Your brother was driving a small sports car, a convertible. When it rolled, he didn't have a chance."

Ty had tried to talk Bruce out of that car, but to no avail. Any kind of advice was unwelcome if it came from big brother. That was one of the by-products of their parents' divorce. Bruce had been raised by their mother, Ty by their father. And the difference in the upbringings was striking, even to outsiders.

The doctor had paused long enough to produce Bruce's personal effects. The soiled clothing was there, along with a handful of change, some keys, and a clip of hundred-dollar bills. Ty looked at them blankly before stuffing them back into the sack.

"What a hell of a waste," Ty said quietly. "He was twenty-eight."

"I'm sorry we couldn't save him," Dr. Lawson repeated softly, sincerely.

Ty nodded, lost in bitter memories and regret. "He couldn't even save himself. Fast cars, fast women, alcohol… They said he wasn't legally drunk." His silver-gray eyes met and held the doctor's in a level gaze.

Dr. Lawson nodded.

"He usually drank far too much," Ty said, staring at the sack. "I tried so damned hard to talk him out of that convertible." He sighed heavily. "I talked until I was blue."

"If you're a religious man, Mr. Wade, I can tell you that I still believe in acts of God. This was one."

Ty searched the other man's eyes. After a minute, he nodded. "Thanks."

It was misting rain outside, cold for Texas in November, but he hardly felt it. All that rushing around, he thought blankly, and for what? To get there too late. All his life, where Bruce was concerned, he'd been too late.

It seemed so unreal to think of Bruce as dead. He and Bruce had been a lot alike in looks, at least. Both were dark and light-eyed, except that Bruce's eyes had been more blue than gray. He'd been six years younger than Ty and shorter, more adventurous, more petted. Bruce had been spoiled with easy living and an abundance of attention from their mother. Ty had been raised by their rancher father, a cold, practical, no-nonsense man who looked upon women as a weakness and brought Ty up to feel the same way. Ironically, it was Erin who'd finally separated Bruce from Ty and the ranch.

Erin. His eyes closed briefly as he pictured her, laughing, running to him, her hair long and black and straight, her elfin face bright with joy, her green eyes twinkling, laughing, as her full, soft lips smiled up at him. He groaned.

He leaned his tall, elegant body against the Lincoln as he lit a cigarette. The flare of the match accentuated his high cheekbones, his aquiline nose, the jut of his chin. There was nothing in his face that a woman would find attractive, and he knew it. He had no illusions about his looks. Perhaps that was why he'd attacked Erin on sight, he reflected. She'd been a model when Bruce met her in nearby San Antonio and brought her home for a weekend visit. Young but already well-known, Erin was destined for greater things. That first day, she'd walked into the Wade house with her elfin face excited and friendly, and Ty had stood like stone in the long hallway and glared at her until the vividness of her expression had faded into uncertainty and, then, disappointment.

She'd been so beautiful. A living illusion. All his

secret dreams of perfection rolled into one flawless, willowy body and exquisitely sculpted face. Then Bruce had put his arm around her and looked at her with unashamed worship, and Ty had felt himself growing cold inside. She'd been Bruce's from the very beginning, a prize he'd brought home to big brother, to fling in his arrogant face.

He took a long draw from the cigarette and stared at its amber tip in the misting rain. How long ago it all seemed! But all of it had taken place in just a year's time. The first meeting, the long weekends when Erin came to the ranch and slept in the guest room in order to observe "the proprieties." Conchita, the housekeeper, had taken to Erin immediately, fussing and bustling over her like a mother hen. And Erin had loved it. Her father was dead, her mother constantly flying off to somewhere in Europe. In many ways, Ty thought, her life had been as unloving and cold as his own.

He took another draw from his cigarette and blew out a thick cloud of smoke, his silvery eyes narrowing with memory as he stared sightlessly at the deserted parking lot. He'd antagonized Erin from the start, picking at her, deliberately making her as uncomfortable as possible. She'd taken that smoldering dislike at face value until one dark, cold night when Bruce had been called out on urgent business. Erin and Ty had been alone in the house, and he'd antagonized her one time too many.

He vividly remembered the look in her green eyes when, after she'd slapped him, he'd jerked her into his hard arms and kissed the breath out of her. Her lips had been like red berries, soft and slightly swollen, her eyes wide and soft and dazed. And to his astonishment, instead of slapping him again, she'd reached up to him, her mouth ardent and sweet, her body clinging like ivy to the strength of his.

It had been like a dream sequence. Her mouth, dark, soft wine under his hard lips; her body, welcoming. Soft cushions on the floor in front of the fireplace, her hushed, ragged breathing as he'd bared her breasts and touched them, her shocked cry as he'd touched her intimately and begun to undress her. But she hadn't stopped him; she hadn't even tried. He remembered her voice in his ear, whispering endearments, her hands tenderly caressing his nape as he'd moved her under him.

He ground his teeth together. He hadn't known, hadn't guessed, that she was a virgin. He'd never forget the tormented sound of her voice, the wide-eyed fear that had met his puzzled downward glance. He'd tried to stop, so shocked that he wasn't even thinking…but she'd held him. No, she'd whispered, it was too late to stop now, the damage was already done. And he'd gone on. He'd been so careful then, so careful not to hurt her any more than he already had. But he'd given her no pleasure. He knew, even though she'd tried not to let him see her disappointment. And

before he could try again, could even begin to show
her any real tenderness, they'd heard Bruce's car
coming up the long driveway. Then, with reality, had
come all the doubts, all the hidden fears. And he'd
laughed, taunting her with her easy surrender. Get out,
he'd said coldly, or Bruce was going to get an earful.
He'd watched her dragging her clothing around her,
white-faced, shaking. He'd watched her leave the
room with tears streaming from her eyes. Like a
nightmare, the pain had only gotten worse. But he'd
had too much pride to back down, to apologize, to
explain what he'd felt and why he'd lied to her about
his motives. And early the next morning, she'd left.

Bruce had hated him for that. He'd guessed what
had happened, and he'd followed Erin to wring the
truth from her. A day later he'd moved out, to live
with a friend in San Antonio. Erin had gone on to a
career in New York; her face had haunted him from
the covers of slick magazines for several weeks.

That night haunted him, too. It had been all of
heaven to have her. And then, all at once, he'd realized that she might see his lack of control for what it
was; that she might realize he was vulnerable with
her and take advantage of it. God forgive him, he'd
even thought she might have planned it that way. And
she was so beautiful; too beautiful to care about an
ugly man, a man so inexperienced at making love.
His father's lectures returned with a vengeance, and
he'd convinced himself in a space of seconds that

he'd been had. She was Bruce's, not his. He could never have her. So it was just as well that he'd let her go out of his life....

Bruce had gotten even, just before he'd left the house for good. He'd told Ty that Erin had hated what Ty had done to her, that his "fumbling attempts at lovemaking" had sickened her. Then he'd walked out triumphantly, leaving Ty so sick and humiliated that he'd finished off a bottle of tequila and spent two days in a stupor.

Erin had come back to the ranch two months later, and it had been Ty she'd wanted to talk to, not Bruce. He'd been coming out of the stables leading a brood mare, and she'd driven up in a little sports car, much like the one Bruce would die in almost six months later....

"I have to talk to you," she said in her soft, clear voice. Her eyes were soft, too; full of secrets.

"What do we have to talk about?" Ty replied, his own tone uncompromising, careless.

"If you'll just listen..." she said, looking at him with an odd kind of pleading in her green eyes.

Against his will, he was drawn to her as she poised there in a green print dress that clung lovingly to every soft line of her high-breasted body, the wind whipping her long black hair around her like a shawl. He forced himself to speak coldly, mockingly.

"Aren't you a vision, baby doll?" His eyes traveled pointedly over her body. "How many men have you had since you left here?"

She flinched. "No...no one," she faltered, as if she hadn't expected the attack. "There hasn't been anyone except you."

He threw back his head and laughed, his eyes as cold as silver in a face like stone. "That's a good one. Just don't set your sights on Bruce," he warned softly. "Maybe my plan backfired, but I can still stop him from marrying you. I don't want someone like you in my family. My God, you've got a mother who makes a professional streetwalker look like a virgin, and your father was little more than a con man who died in prison! It'd make me sick to have to introduce you into our circle of friends."

Her face paled, her eyes lost their softness. "I can't help what my people were," she said quietly. "But you've got to listen to me! That night..."

"What about it?" he demanded, his voice faintly bored. "I'd planned to seduce you and then tell Bruce, but you left without forcing my hand. So, no harm done." To avoid looking at her, he bent his head to light a cigarette. Then he glanced up, his eyes narrowed and ugly. "You were just a one-night stand, honey. And one night was enough."

That brought her to tears, and he felt a pain like a knife going into his gut despite the fact that he was justified in that lie. She'd told it all to Bruce, hadn't she? "What a sacrifice it must have been for you," she whispered in anguish. "I must have been a terrible disappointment."

"I'll amen that," he told her. "You were a total failure, weren't you? Why did you come down here, anyway? Bruce doesn't come here anymore, and don't pretend you don't know it."

"I'm not looking for Bruce," she burst out. "Oh, Ty, I haven't seen him since I left here! It's you I came to see. There's something I've got to tell you…!"

"I've got livestock to look after," he said indifferently, dismissing her. "Get out of here. Go model a gown or something."

Her eyes grew dull then; something died in them. She looked at him for a long, quiet moment, almost said something else; then, as if defeated, turned away.

"Just a minute," he called after her.

She'd turned, an expression of hope on her face. "Yes?"

He smiled down at her mockingly, forcing himself not to weaken, not to let her get the best of him. "If you came to see me because you wanted another roll in the hay, I'll let the cattle wait for a few minutes," he offered. "Maybe you've improved since the last time."

Her eyes closed, her face contorted as if in pain. "How could you, Tyson?" she whispered, then opened her eyes to reveal an anguish so profound that Ty was forced to look away. But the agony in her voice pierced his soul. "How could you? Oh, God, you don't know how much I...!"

Almost. He almost abandoned his lacerated pride and went to her. His feet even started to move. But suddenly, she whirled and ran to her car, gunned it to life and raced frantically down the long drive, sending the small convertible sliding on the gravel as she shot it out onto the paved road. He watched the car until it was out of sight, feeling empty and cold and lonely....

That was the last time he'd seen Erin Scott. And now Bruce was dead. He wondered if she'd still been seeing his brother. Bruce hadn't mentioned her. Of course, he'd hardly spoken to Ty in all those months. That had hurt, too. Lately, just about everything did.

He crushed out the cigarette. There were funeral arrangements to make. He thought about the room-mate Bruce had moved in with and wondered if he knew. He got into the car and went directly to the apartment. It might help to talk to someone who knew Bruce, who could tell him if Bruce had ever forgiven him for driving Erin away. It was very nearly a need for absolution, but Tyson Wade would never have admitted it. Not even to himself.

Two

Bruce's roommate was a rather shy accountant, a nice man without complexities and as pleasant as Bruce had always been. He was drinking heavily when Ty entered the apartment.

"I'm so sorry," Sam Harris said with genuine feeling, raking back his sandy-blond hair. "I heard it on television just a few minutes ago. God, I'm so sorry. He was a great guy."

"Yes," Ty said quietly. He stuck his hands in his pockets and looked around the small apartment. There was nothing to indicate that Bruce had ever lived there except a large photograph of Erin in a swimsuit pose beside one of the twin beds. Ty felt himself stiffening at the sight of it.

"Poor old guy," Sam said wearily, sinking down onto the sofa with a shot glass in his hands. "He worshiped that girl, but she never even let him get close." He nodded toward the bed. "There's a whole box of letters she sent back last week under there."

Ty's heart froze. "Letters?"

"Sure." Sam pulled them out. There were dozens, all from Bruce, all addressed to Erin. All unopened. And there was one letter, from her, to Bruce. It was very recent. And opened.

"He went crazy when he read that last one," Sam told him. "Just hog wild. I never had the nerve to sneak a look at it. And he changed after that. Raged about you, Mr. Wade," he added apologetically. "He changed his will, made all kinds of threats.... I almost called you, but I figured it really wasn't any of my business. And you know how Bruce got when he thought someone had sold him out. He was my pal, after all."

Ty stared at the letters in his hand, feeling sick all over.

"There are some things of his in the drawers, too." Sam gestured aimlessly, then sat down again. "I keep looking for him, you know," he murmured absently. "I keep thinking, any minute he'll open the door and walk in."

"If you'll pack his things, when you get a chance," Ty said quietly, "I'll send for them."

"Sure, I'll be glad to. I'd like to come to the funeral," he added.

Ty nodded. "You can serve as a pallbearer if you like," he said. "It'll be at the First Presbyterian Church, day after tomorrow. There aren't any living relatives, except me."

"God, I'm sorry," Sam repeated hollowly.

Ty hesitated, then shrugged his broad shoulders. "So am I. Good night."

Just like that. He walked out, clutching the box of letters in his hands, more apprehensive than he'd ever been in his life. Part of him was afraid of what might be in them.

Two hours later, he was sitting in his pine-paneled den at Staghorn with a half-empty bottle of whiskey in one hand and a much used glass in the other. His eyes were cold and bitter, and he was numb with the pain of discovery.

The letters Bruce had written to Erin were full of unrequited love, brimming with passion and proposals of marriage and plans that all included her. Each was more ardent than the one before. And in every one was at least one sentence about Ty and how much he hated her.

Those were bad enough. But the letter Erin had sent to Bruce tore at his heart.

"Dearest Bruce," she'd written in a fine, delicate, hand, "I am returning all your letters, in hopes that they will make you realize that I can't give you what you want from me. You're a fine man, and any woman would be lucky to marry you. But I can't love you, Bruce. I never have, and I never can. Even if things were different between us, any sort of relationship would be impossible because of your brother.'' His heart leaped and then froze as he read on: ''Even though the fault was partially mine, I can't forget or forgive what's happened to me. I've been through two surgeries now, one to put a steel rod in my crushed pelvis, the other to remove it. I walk with a cane, and I'm scarred. Perhaps the emotional scars are even worse, since I lost the baby in the wreck, too....''

The baby! Ty's eyes closed and his body shook with anguish. He couldn't finish the letter. She'd left Staghorn hell-bent for leather, and she'd wrecked the car. Her pelvis had been crushed. She'd lost the baby she was carrying, she'd been hospitalized, she'd even lost her career. All because of him. Because Bruce had told him a lie, and he'd believed it. And now Bruce was dead, and Erin was crippled and bitter, hating him. Blaming him. And he blamed himself, too. He hurt as he'd never hurt in his life.

And now he knew why she'd come to see him. She'd been carrying his child. She was going to tell him. But he hadn't let her. He'd humiliated her into leaving. And because of him, she'd lost everything.

The baby would haunt him all his life, he knew. He'd never had anyone of his own, anything to love or protect or take care of. Except Bruce. And Bruce had been too old for that kind of babying. Ty had wanted someone to spoil, someone to give things to and look after. And he'd tried to make Bruce into the child he himself would never have. But there had been a child. And obviously Erin had planned to keep it. His child. He remembered now, too late, the hopeful look in her eyes, the softness of her expression when she'd said, "I have something to tell you...."

His hand opened, letting the letter drop to the floor. He poured out another measure of whiskey and downed some of it quickly, feeling a tightness in his chest that would not, he knew, be eased by liquor.

He stared helplessly at the whiskey bottle for a long time. Then he got slowly to his feet, still staring at it, his face contorted with grief and rage. And he flung it at the fireplace with the full strength of his long, muscular arm, watched as it shattered against the bricks, watched the flames hit the alcohol and shoot up into the blackened chimney.

"Erin," he whispered brokenly. "Oh, God, Erin, forgive me!"

The sudden opening of the door startled him. He didn't turn, mindful of the glaze over his eyes, the fixed rigidity of his face.

"Yes?" he demanded coldly.

"Señor Ty, are you all right?" Conchita asked gently.

His shoulders shifted. "Yes."

"Can I bring you something to eat?"

He shook his head. "Tell José I need five pall-bearers," he said. "Bruce's roommate asked to be one already."

"*Si, señor.* You have talked with the minister?"

"I did that when I came home."

"Are you sure that I cannot bring you something?" the middle-aged Spanish woman asked softly.

"Absolution," he said, his voice ghostly, haunted. "Only that."

It was three days before Ty began to surface from his emotional torment. The funeral was held in the cold rain, with only the men and Bruce's roommate to mourn him. Ty had thought about contacting Erin, but if she'd just been released from the hospital, she wouldn't be in any condition to come to a funeral. He wanted to call her, to talk with her. But he didn't want to hurt her anymore. His voice would bring back too many memories, open too many wounds. She'd never believe how much he regretted what he'd done. She probably wouldn't even listen. So what was the use of upsetting her?

He went into town after the funeral to see Ed Johnson, the family's attorney. With the strain between himself and his brother, Ty expected that Bruce had tried to keep him from inheriting his share of Staghorn—an assumption that proved to be all too true.

Ed was pushing fifty and balding, with a warm personality and a keen wit. He rose as Ty entered his office and held out his hand.

"I saw you at the funeral," he said solemnly, "but I didn't want to intrude. I figured you'd be in to see me."

Ty took off his cream-colored Stetson and sat down, crossing his long legs. He looked elegant in his blue pinstriped suit, every inch the cattle king. His silver eyes pinned the attorney as he waited silently for the older man to speak.

"Bruce has changed his will three times in the past year," Ed began. "Once, he tried to borrow money on the estate for some get-rich-quick scheme. He was so changeable. And after last week, I feared for his sanity."

Last week. Just after he'd received Erin's letter. Poor boy, Ty thought. He closed his eyes and sighed. "He cut me out of his will, obviously," he said matter-of-factly.

"Got it in one," Ed replied. "He left everything he had to a woman with a New York address. I think it's that model he was dating a few months back," he mumbled, missing Ty's shocked expression. "Yes, here it is. Miss Erin Scott. His entire holdings. With the provision," he added, lifting his eyes to Ty's white face, "that she come and live on the ranch. If she doesn't meet that condition, every penny of his holdings goes to Ward Jessup."

Ward Jessup! Ty's breath caught in his throat. He

and Ward Jessup were long-standing enemies. Jessup's ranch, which adjoined Staghorn, was littered with oil rigs, and the man made no secret of the fact that he wanted to extend his oil search to the portion of Staghorn closest to his land. Although Ty had been adamant about not selling, Jessup had made several attempts to persuade Bruce to sell to him. And now, if Erin refused to come, he'd have his way—he'd have half of Staghorn. What a priceless piece of revenge, Ty thought absently. Because Bruce knew how much Erin hated Ty—that she'd rather die than share a roof with Tyson Wade—he'd made sure big brother would never inherit.

"That's the end of it, I guess," Ty said gently.

"I don't understand." Ed stared at him over his glasses.

"Bruce had a letter from her last week," the younger man said, his voice level, quiet. "She was in a wreck some time ago. She's been crippled, and she lost the child she was carrying. I'm responsible."

"Was it Bruce's child?"

Ty met the curious stare levelly. "No. It was mine."

Ed cleared his throat. "Oh. I'm sorry."

"Not half as sorry as I am," he said, and got up. "Thanks for your time, Ed."

"Wait a minute," the attorney said. "You aren't just giving up half your ranch, for God's sake? Not after you've worked most of your life to build it into what it is?''

Ty stared at him. "Erin hates me. I can't imagine that she'd be charitable enough to want to help me, not after the way I've treated her. She has more reason than Bruce to want revenge. And I don't have much heart for a fight, not even to save Staghorn. One way or another, it's been a hell of a week.'' He jammed his Stetson down over his hair, his eyes lifeless. "If she wants to cut my throat, I'm going to let her. My God, that's the least I owe her!''

Ed watched him leave, frowning. That didn't sound like the Tyson Wade he knew. Something had changed him, perhaps losing his brother. The old Ty would have fought with his last breath to save the homestead. Ed shook his head and picked up the phone.

"Jennie, get me Erin Scott in New York,'' he told his secretary, and gave her the number. Seconds later a pleasant, ladylike voice came on the line.

"Yes?''

"Miss Scott?'' he asked.

"I'm Erin Scott.''

"I'm Edward Johnson in Ravine, Texas…the attorney for the Wade family,'' he clarified.

"I haven't asked for restitution—''

"It's about a totally different matter, Miss Scott,'' he interrupted. "You knew my client, Bruce Wade?''

There was a long pause. "Bruce...has something happened to him?"

"He was in an automobile accident three days ago, Miss Scott. I'm sorry to have to tell you that it was fatal."

"Oh." She sighed. "Oh. I'm very sorry, Mr....?"

"Johnson. Ed Johnson. I'm calling to inform you that he named you his beneficiary."

"Beneficiary?"

She sounded stunned. He supposed she was. "Miss Scott, you inherit a substantial amount of cash in the bequest, as well as part ownership of the Staghorn ranch."

"I can't believe he did that," she murmured. "I can't believe it! What about his brother?"

"I don't quite understand the situation, I admit, but the will is ironclad. You inherit. With a small proviso, that is," he added reluctantly.

"What proviso?"

"That you live on the ranch."

"Never!" she spat.

So Ty was right. He leaned back in his chair. "I expected that reaction," he told her. "But you'd better hear the rest of it.... Miss Scott?"

"I'm still here." Her voice was shaking.

"If you don't meet that provision," he said, his voice steady, even a little impatient, "your half of the ranch will go to Ward Jessup."

There was a long silence. "That's Ty's...Mr. Wade's...neighbor," she recalled.

"That's right. And, I might add, something of an adversary. He only wants the oil rights to Staghorn, you know. He'd sell off the stock. The ranch couldn't survive with what would be left. There are several families whose sole support is Staghorn—a blacksmith, several cowhands, a veterinarian, a storekeeper, a mechanic—"

"I...know how big the place is," Erin said quietly. "Some of those people have worked for the Wades for three generations."

"That's correct." He was amazed that she knew so much about Staghorn.

"I need time to think," she said after a pause. "I've just come out of the hospital, Mr. Johnson. It's very difficult for me to walk at all. A trip of that kind would be extremely hard on me."

"Mr. Wade has a private plane," he reminded her.

"I don't know..."

"The terms of the will are very explicit," he said. "And they require immediate action. I'm sorry. I need an answer today."

There was another long pause. "Tell Mr. Wade... I'll come."

Ed had to force himself not to grin.

"There's just one thing," she said hesitantly. "How long must I stay there?"

"No particular length of time was specified," he

told her. "That leaves it to the interpretation of the people involved. And believe me, Mr. Jessup will interpret it to mean until you die."

"I've heard that he's quite ruthless." She sighed. "I guess I'll cross that bridge when I come to it. I can be ready tomorrow afternoon, Mr. Johnson."

She sounded tired, and in pain. He felt guilty for pressing her, but he knew it couldn't have waited.

"I'll pass that information along. Meanwhile, Miss Scott, I'll get the necessary paperwork done. You're quite a wealthy young woman now."

"Quite wealthy," she repeated dully, and hung up.

She was sitting on a sofa that swayed almost to the floor, in a ground-floor apartment in Queens. The water was mostly cold, the heating worked only occasionally. She was wrapped in a thick old coat to keep warm, and no one who'd known her six months ago would recognize her.

Why had she agreed to go? she wondered miserably. She was in pain already, and all she'd done today was go back and forth to the bathroom. Her leg was giving her hell. They'd showed her the exercises, stressing that she must do them twice a day, religiously, or she'd never lose her limp. A limping model was not exactly employable, she reminded herself. But there seemed so little point in it all now. She'd lost everything. She had no future to look forward to, nothing to live for. Nothing except revenge. And even that left a bad taste in her mouth.

She couldn't see those people out of work, she thought. Not in winter, which November practically was. She couldn't stand by and leave them homeless and jobless because of her.

She stretched out her leg, grimacing as the muscles protested. Exercises indeed! It was hard enough to walk, let alone do lifts and such. Her eyes were drawn to the window. Outside, it was raining. She wondered if it was raining in Ravine, Texas, and what Tyson Wade was doing right now. Would he be cursing her for all he was worth? Probably. He'd been sure that she'd never set foot on Staghorn again, after the things he'd said to her. He wouldn't know about the accident, of course, or the baby. She felt her eyes go cold. If only she could hurt him as badly as he'd hurt her. If only!

She could stay here, of course. She could change her mind, refuse the conditions of the inheritance. Sure. And she could fly, too. All those people, some of them with children, all out in the cold…

She lay back down on the sofa and closed her eyes. There would be time enough to worry about it later. Now, she only wanted to sleep and forget.

Ty. She was running toward him, her arms out-stretched, and he was laughing, waiting for her. He lifted her up against him and kissed her with aching tenderness. He stared down at her, his eyes filled with love. She was pregnant, very pregnant, and he was

touching the mound of her belly, his hands possessive, his eyes adoring....

She awoke with tears in her eyes. Always it was
the same dream, with the same ending. Always she
woke crying. She got up and washed her face, looking
at the clock. Bedtime already. She'd slept for hours.
She pulled on a cotton gown and went to bed, taking
a sleeping pill before she lay down. Perhaps this time,
she wouldn't dream.

By early the next afternoon, she was packed and
waiting for whomever Tyson sent to get her. Her once
elegant suitcase was sitting by the door, filled with
her meager wardrobe. She was wearing a simple beige
knit suit that would have fit her six months ago. Now
it hung on her, making her look almost skeletal. Her
lusterless hair was tied in a bun, her face devoid of
makeup. In her right hand was a heavy cane, dangling
beside the leg that still refused to support her.

At two o'clock precisely, there came a knock on
the door. "Come in," she called from the sofa, only
vaguely curious about which poor soul Ty would have
sacrificed to come and fly her down to Texas.

She got the shock of her life when the door opened
to admit Tyson Wade himself.

He stopped dead in the doorway and stared at her
as she got unsteadily to her feet, leaning heavily on
the cane. The impact of his handiwork was damning.

He remembered a laughing young girl. Here was
an old, tired woman with green eyes that held no life

at all, no gaiety…only a resigned kind of pain. She was pitifully thin, and her face was pale and drawn. She stared at him as if he were a stranger, and perhaps he was. Perhaps he always had been, because he'd never really let her get close enough to know him in any way but one.

"Hello, Erin," he said quietly.

She inclined her head. "Hello, Tyson," she said.

He looked around him with obvious distaste, his silver eyes reflecting his feelings about her surroundings.

"I haven't been able to work for several months," she informed him. "I've been drawing a disability pension and eating thanks to food stamps."

His eyes closed briefly; when they opened, they were vaguely haunted. "You won't have to live on food stamps now," he said, his voice rough.

"Obviously not, according to your family attorney." She smiled faintly. "I imagined you screaming at the top of your lungs for an hour, trying to find a way to break the will."

He studied her wan, sad little face. "Are you ready to go?" he asked.

She shrugged. "Lead on. You'll have to allow for my leg. I don't move so quickly these days."

He watched her come toward him, every movement careful and obviously painful.

"Oh, my God," he said tightly.

Her eyes flared at him. "Don't pity me," she hissed. "Don't you dare!"

His chin lifted as he took a long, slow breath. "How bad is it?" he asked.

She stopped just in front of him. "I'll make it," she said coldly.

He only nodded. He turned to open the door, holding it as she brushed against him. She smelled of roses, and as he caught the scent in his nostrils, he struggled to suppress memories that were scarcely bearable.

"Erin," he said huskily as she went past him.

But she didn't answer him, she didn't look at him. She moved painfully down the hall and out the open door to the street. She didn't even look back.

After a minute, he picked up her suitcase, locked the door, and followed her.

Three

It was all Ty could do to keep silent as he and Erin rode to the airport. There were so many things he wanted to say to her, to explain, to discuss. He wanted to apologize, but that was impossible for him. Odd, he thought, how much heartache pride had caused him over the years. He'd never learned to bend. His father had taught him that a man never could, and still call himself a man.

He lit a cigarette and smoked it silently, only half aware of Erin's quiet scrutiny as he weaved easily through the frantic city traffic. His nerve never wavered. Texas or New York, he was at home in a car even in the roughest traffic.

"Nothing bothers you, does it?" she asked carelessly.

"Don't you believe it," he replied. He glanced at her, his eyes steady and curious as he waited at a traffic light.

"Six months," she murmured, her voice as devoid of feeling as the green eyes that seemed to look right through him. "So much can happen in just six months."

Ty averted his eyes. "Yes." He studied the traffic light intently. It was easier than seeing that closed, unfeeling look on her face, and knowing that he was responsible for it. Once, she'd have run toward him laughing....

She turned the cane in her hands, feeling its coolness. Ty seemed different somehow. Less arrogant, less callous. Perhaps his brother's death had caused that change, although he and Bruce had never been close. She wondered if he blamed her for his estrangement from Bruce, if he knew how insanely jealous Bruce had been of her, and without any cause at all.

He watched her toying with the cane as he pulled back into the flow of traffic and crossed the bridge that would take them to the airport. "How long will you have to use that thing?" he asked conversationally.

"I don't know." She did know. They'd told her. If she didn't do the exercises religiously, she'd be using it for the rest of her life. But what did that matter now? She could never go back to modeling. And nothing else seemed to be worth the effort.

"I didn't expect you to agree to the stipulation in Bruce's will," he said suddenly.

"No, I don't imagine you did." She glared at him. "What's the matter, cattle baron, did you expect that I'd sit on my pride and let your whole crew lose their jobs on my account?"

So that was why. It had nothing to do with any remaining feeling for him; it was to help someone less fortunate. He should have known.

"You look surprised," she observed.

"Not really." He pulled into the rental car lot at the airport and stopped the car, then turned toward her. "You were always generous—" his silver eyes held hers relentlessly "—in every way."

Her face colored, and she jerked her eyes away. She couldn't bear to remember…that!

"It wasn't an insult," he said quickly. "Don't… don't make it personal."

She laughed through stinging tears, a young animal at bay, glaring at him from the corner of her seat. "Personal! Don't make it personal? Look at me, damn you!" she cried.

His hand reached toward her, or seemed to, and suddenly retracted, along with any show of emotion that might have softened the hard lines of his face. He stared at his smoking cigarette, took a last draw with damnably steady fingers, and put it out carefully in the ashtray.

"I've been looking," he said quietly, lifting his eyes. "Every second since I've been with you. Would you like to know what I see?"

"How about a burned-out shell; does that cover it?" she said defiantly.

"You've given up, haven't you?" he said. "You've stopped living, you've stopped working, you've stopped caring."

"I have a right!"

"You have every right," he agreed shortly. "I'd be the first to agree with that. But for God's sake, woman, look what you're doing to yourself! Do you want to end up a cripple?"

"I *am* a cripple!"

"Only in your mind," he replied, his voice deliberately sharp. "You've convinced yourself that your life is over; that you can come down to Staghorn and draw into some kind of shell and just exist while everyone else prospers. But you're wrong, lady. Because that's something you'll never do. I'm going to make you start living again. You're going to pick up the pieces and start over. I'll see to it."

"Like hell you will, Tyson Almighty Wade!"

"If you come back with me, you can count on it," he replied. He put a long hard arm over the back of the seat, and his silver eyes glittered at her, challenging, taunting. "Come on, Erin. Tell me to take my money and go to hell. Tell me to give Ward Jessup your half of the spread and put all those workers on unemployment.''

She wanted to. Oh, how she wanted to! But it was more than her conscience could bear. She glared at him out of a white face in its frame of soft dark hair, her green eyes alive now, burning in anger. ''I hate you!'' she cried.

''I know,'' he replied. His eyes narrowed. ''I don't blame you for that. You have the right. I'd never have asked you to come back.''

''No, not you.'' She smiled coldly. ''But if I hadn't, you'd probably have come rushing up here to kidnap me and take me back by force.''

He shook his head. ''Not now. Not after what's happened.'' He let his eyes wander slowly over her frail body.

She eyed him warily. ''Mr. Johnson told you about the wreck, I suppose?''

He looked down at the cane. ''I read your last letter to Bruce,'' he said in a voice that was deep and quiet…and frankly haunted.

Her spirit broke at his tone. She could take anything from him except tenderness. Guilt. His. Hers. Bruce's. And none of it any use. A tortured sob burst from her throat. She tried to stifle it but couldn't.

His eyes lifted, holding hers. ''I wish I could tell you how I felt when I knew,'' he said hesitantly. ''The things I said to you that day…''

She swallowed, slowly gaining control of herself. "You...you meant them," she replied. "Reliving them isn't going to do any good now. You saved Bruce from me. That's all you cared about."

"No!" he said huskily. "No, that's wrong."

He started to reach toward her, and she backed away until the door stopped her.

"Don't you touch me," she said in a high, strangled voice. "Don't you ever touch me again. If you do, I'll walk out the door, and you and your outfit can all go to hell!"

His face closed up. It was the first time he'd ever reached out toward her, and her rejection hurt. But he struggled against familiar feelings of wounded pride, struggled to understand things from her side. He'd hurt her brutally. It was going to take time, a lot of it, before she'd begin to trust him. Well, he had time. Right now, that and the hope that she might someday stop hating him were all he had.

"Okay," he said, his voice steady, almost tender. "Want something to eat before we get on the plane?"

She shifted restlessly, staring at him, eyes huge in her thin face. "I...didn't have lunch," she faltered.

"We'll get a sandwich, then." He got out and went around to open her door. But he didn't offer to help her. He watched her put the cane down and lean on it heavily. "How long has it been since they took out the rod?" he asked.

Her eyes widened. She hadn't realized he knew so

much about her condition. "A couple of weeks," she told him.

"Were you taking physical therapy?"

She avoided his probing look. "I could use some coffee."

"Therapy," he persisted, "is the only way you'll ever walk without a cane. Did they tell you that?"

"You've got a lot of nerve...!" She glared up at him.

"I busted my hip on the rodeo circuit when I was twenty-four," he told her flatly. "It was months before I stopped limping, and physical therapy was the only thing that saved me from a stiff leg. I remember the exercises to this day, and how they're done, and how long for each day. So I'll help you get into the routine."

"I'll help you into the hospital if you try it," she threatened.

"Spunky," he approved, nodding. He even smiled a little. "You always were. I liked that about you, from the very beginning."

"You liked nothing about me," she reminded him. "You hated me on sight, and from there it was all downhill."

"Are you sure?" he asked, watching her curiously. "I thought women had instincts about men and their reactions."

"As you found out the hard way, I knew very little about men. Then."

He didn't look away. "And as you found out, the hard way, I knew very little about women."

She flinched, just a little, then searched that gray fog in his eyes, wondering what he meant. It sounded like a confession of sorts, but it just didn't jibe with the picture Bruce had painted of him—a womanizer with a reputation as long as her arm.

"Pull the other one," she said finally. "You've probably forgotten more about women than I'll ever know. Bruce said you had."

His jaw tensed. "Bruce said one hell of a lot, didn't he? I heard what you thought of my 'fumbling,' too."

She stiffened and froze. "What?"

"He said you thought I was a clumsy, fumbling fool. That you described it all to him, and laughed together about it...."

Her lips parted, and her face went stark white. "He told you...he said that...to you?"

"Erin!" He leaped forward just in time to catch her as she collapsed. He lifted her, feeling the pitiful weight of her in his arms, feeling alive for the first time in months. He held her close, bending his head over hers, drowning in the bittersweet anguish of holding her while all around them traffic moved routinely and tourists milled indifferently on the sidewalks.

"Baby," he whispered softly, cradling her in his hard arms as he dropped into the passenger seat of the car and looked down at her. He smoothed the hair from her face, caressing her pale cheek with a trembling hand. "Erin."

Her eyes opened a minute later. She blinked, and for an instant—for one staggering second—her eyes were unguarded and full of memories. And then it was like watching a curtain come down. The instant she recognized him, all the life went out of her face.

"You fainted," he said gently.

She stared up at him dizzily, feeling his warmth and strength, catching the scent of leather that clung to him like the spicy after-shave he favored.

"Ty," she whispered.

His heart stopped and then raced, and his body made a sudden and shocking statement about its immediate needs. He shifted her quickly, careful not to let her know how vulnerable he was.

"Are you all right?" he asked.

She leaned her forehead against his shoulder. "I feel a little shaky, that's all."

He touched her hair, on fire with the sweetness of her being near, loving the smell of roses that clung to her, the warmth of her soft body against his.

"Bruce didn't say that to you—" she shook her head "—he couldn't have!" There were tears in her eyes.

"I shouldn't have said anything," he mumbled. "I didn't mean to. Here, are you all right now?"

She sighed heavily. It was a lie. A lie. She'd never said any such thing to Bruce. She looked up into watchful gray eyes and tried to speak, but she was lost in the sudden electricity that arced between them.

"Your eyes always reminded me of green velvet," he said absently, searching them. "Soft and rippling in the light, full of hidden softness and warmth."

Her breath was trapped somewhere, and she couldn't seem to free it. Her eyes wandered over his homely face, seeing the new lines, the angles and craggy roughness, the strength.

"You won't find beauty even if you look hard," he said in a tone that was almost but not quite amused.

"You were so different from Bruce," she whispered. "Always so different. Remote and alone and invulnerable."

"Except for one long night," he agreed, watching the color return to her cheeks. "Will you at least believe that I regret what I did to you? That if I could take it all back, I would?"

"Looking back won't change anything," she said wearily, and closed her eyes. "Oh, Ty, it won't change anything at all."

"I'm sorry…about the baby we made," he said hesitantly, his voice husky with emotion.

She looked up at him, startled by his tone. She saw something there, something elusive. "You would have wanted it," she said with sudden insight.

He nodded. "If I'd known, I'd never have let you go."

It was the way he said it, with such aching feeling. She realized that he meant it. Perhaps he'd wanted a family of his own, perhaps there had been a woman he'd wanted and couldn't have. Maybe he'd thought about having children of his own and taking care of them. He wasn't anything to look at; that was a fact. But he might have been vulnerable once. He might have been capable of love and tenderness and warmth. A hundred years ago, judging by the walls he'd raised around himself.

She looked away and struggled to get up. He let her go instantly, helping her to her feet, steadying her with hands that were unexpectedly gentle. Guilt, she thought, glancing at him. He was capable of that, at least. But guilt was one thing she didn't want from him. Or pity.

"I'm all right now," she said, easing away from him. The closeness of his body had affected her in ways she didn't want to remember. She'd given herself to him that night with such eager abandon. With joy. Because she'd loved him desperately, and she'd thought that he loved her. But it had only been a lie, a trick. Could she ever forget that?

"It's all right," he said gently, oblivious to the curious stares of passersby, who found it oddly evocative to see the thin, crippled young woman being comforted by the tall, strong man.

"I'm so tired," she whispered wearily. "So tired."

He could see that. Thinking about all she'd been

through made him feel curiously protective. He touched her hair in a hesitant gesture. "You'll be all right," he said quietly. "I'll take care of you. I'll take care of everything now." He straightened. "Come on. Let's go home."

It wasn't home, but she was too exhausted to struggle with him. She only wanted a place to rest and a little peace. So much had happened to her that she felt like a victim of delayed shock. She couldn't cope just yet with the memories or the future. She wanted to close her eyes and forget that either even existed.

Ty took her arm to lead her toward the tarmac, and she followed him without protest.

That simple action hit him so hard that his face would have shocked her, had she been able to see it. Erin had always been a fighter, a little firecracker. He'd admired her spirit even as he'd searched for ways to beat it out of her. And now, to see her this way, to know that she was defeated…was profoundly disturbing. She'd been crippled, had lost the baby he'd given her, and he knew that she could never forgive him. He wondered if he could forgive himself. He only knew that he was going to see to it that she left Staghorn whole again, no matter what it took. He was going to give her life back to her, regardless of the cost. He was going to make her well enough to walk away from him.

And he hadn't realized until that moment that it was going to hurt like hell.

* * *

The plane was a big twin-engine Cessna, a pretty bird built for comfort and speed. There was more than enough room for Erin to sit or stretch out in the passenger space, but she wanted to see where she was going.

"Could I sit up front with you?" she asked.

It was the first bit of enthusiasm she'd shown since he'd found her at the apartment. "Of course," he replied. He ushered her into the seat beside his and helped her with the seat belt and the earphones.

She watched, fascinated, as he readied the big plane for takeoff and called the tower for permission to taxi. She'd never flown in his private plane before, although Bruce had invited her once. Ty had objected at the time, finding some reason why she couldn't go with them. He'd never wanted her along. He'd never wanted her near him at all.

He flew with a minimum of conversation, intent on the controls and instrument readings. He asked her once if she was comfortable enough, and that was the only thing he said all the way back to Staghorn.

The ranch was just as Erin remembered it—big and sprawling and like a small town unto itself. The house was a creamy yellow Spanish stucco with a red roof, graceful arches and cacti landscaping all around it. Nearby were the ultramodern stables and corrals and an embryo transplant center second to none in the area. Ty's genius for keeping up with new techniques, his willingness to entertain new methods of production, were responsible for the ranch's amazing climb from a small holding to an empire. It wasn't really surprising that he was so good with figures, though. He was geared to business, to making money. He was good at it because it was his life. He enjoyed the challenge of business in ways he'd never been able to enjoy anything else. Especially personal relationships.

Erin was fascinated by how little the ranch had changed since she'd seen it last. In her world, people came and went. But in Ty's there was consistency. Security. At Staghorn, very little changed. The household staff, of course, was the same. Conchita and her husband, José, were still looking after the *señor*, keeping everything in exquisite order both inside and out. They were middle-aged, and their parents had worked for *el grande señor*, Ty's father, Norman.

Conchita was tall and elegant, very thin, with snapping dark eyes that held the most mischievous twinkle despite the gray that salted her thick black hair. José was just her height, with the same elegant darkness, but his hair had already gone silver. Rumor had it that Señor Norman himself had turned it silver with his temper. José was unfailingly good-natured, and such a good hand with horses that Ty frequently let him work with the horse wrangler.

The house had two stories, but it was on the ground floor that Erin's room was located. Only two doors

away from Ty's. That was vaguely disquieting, but
Erin was sure that he'd only put her on the ground
floor because of her hip.

"If you need anything, there's a pull rope by the
bed." Ty showed it to her. "Conchita will hear you,
night or day. Or I will."

She sat down gingerly in a wing chair by the lacy
curtains of the window and closed her eyes with a
sigh. "Thank you."

He didn't leave. He perched himself on the spotless
white coverlet of the bed and stared at her for a long
moment.

"You're not well," he said at last.

"You try going through two major surgeries in six
months and see how well you are," she returned without opening her eyes.

"I want you to see my family doctor. Let him pre-
scribe some exercises for that hip."

Her eyes opened, accusing. "Now look here. It's
my hip, and my life, and I'll decide—"

"Not while you're on Staghorn, you won't." He
stood up. "Your color isn't good. I want you seen
to."

"I'm not your responsibility...."

Arguing did no good. He simply ignored whatever
she said. "I'll make an appointment for you," he
said, studying her. "Maybe he can give you some
vitamins, too. You're awfully damned thin."

"Ty..."

"Lie down and rest for a while. I'll have Conchita make you some hot chocolate. That should warm you up and put you to sleep as well. The thermostat's over here, if it gets too cold for you." He indicated the dial on the wall near the door.

"Will you stop ordering me around!" she burst out, exasperated.

He studied her face, seeing the sudden color in it, the missing vitality. "That's better." He nodded. "Now you look halfway human again."

Her eyes sparked at him. "I don't know why I came here!"

"Sure you do. You've saving my people from bankruptcy." He opened the door. "Ring if you want anything."

"I want…" She lowered her voice. "I'd like to go and see Bruce's grave."

His face didn't change, but it seemed almost to soften. "I'll take you out there later. When you've had time to rest."

She studied his face, musing that nothing ever showed on that hard countenance. If he had emotions, they were deeply hidden.

"Do you miss him?" she asked curiously.

He turned. "I'll have José bring your suitcase in later."

He closed the door behind him. Yes, he thought bitterly as he moved off down the hall. He missed his brother. But he missed what he'd lost even more: he missed the life he could have had with Erin. Christmas was only a month away, and he was tormented by images of how he might have been celebrating it if Bruce hadn't poisoned his mind. It seemed such a short time ago that Erin had come running toward him, laughing, her black hair like silk around an elfin face. And he'd melted inside just at the sight of her, gone breathless like a boy with his first real date. It still felt like that, despite her scars, her limp. In his heart, he carried a portrait of her that would withstand all the long, aging years, that would leave her young and unscarred for as long as he lived. Erin. How beautiful life might have been, if only...

He made a rough sound in his throat and went quickly out the front door.

Bruce was buried in a quiet country cemetery just ten minutes' drive from Staghorn. Erin stood over his grave while Ty sat in his big Lincoln smoking a cigarette and watching her.

It was sad, Erin thought, the way Bruce had ended his life. He'd never seemed reckless. At least not until he'd started dating her. Once she'd realized that he was expecting more than she could give, she'd eased away from him. She hadn't known how competitive he was with Ty, or that he'd only been using her as a tool of revenge against the elder brother who dominated him. She'd been his crowning glory, his mark of achievement. Look, he'd said without words, showing her proudly to Ty, look what a beauty I brought home. And she's all mine.

She smiled wistfully. She'd been blissfully unaware of the fact that Ty's father and mother had separated years ago and that each had taken one of the boys. Norman Wade had raised Ty, without the weakness of love to make him vulnerable. Ty's mother had raised Bruce, making sure that he was protected from life. The outcome in both cases had been predictable—but not to the parents.

She glanced at the other graves in the plot where Bruce was buried. His parents were there. Norman and Camilla Harding Wade. Side by side in death, as they'd been unable to remain in life. Oddly enough, despite all their difference, they'd shared a deep and lasting love. Neither of them had ever dated after their separation. And it was the last request of each that they be buried together. Erin felt tears burn her eyes as she stared at the single tombstone that marked both their graves. Love like that had to be a rare thing. She wondered why it had all gone wrong for them.

Ty, sensing the questions, got leisurely out of the car and came toward her. He was back in his familiar denims, with high leather boots and the beaten-up tan Stetson he'd worn ever since she'd known him.

"Why couldn't they live together?" she asked him, curious.

He shrugged. "He was a cold man, she was a hot woman," he said succinctly. "That says everything."

She flushed as the meaning penetrated, and averted her eyes.

"What brought that on?" he murmured, and actually started to smile. "I only meant he never showed his feelings, and she wore hers on her sleeve. I don't know how they were in bed. I never asked."

The blush deepened. "Will you stop that?" she muttered.

"And I thought I was old-fashioned," he said. He took a draw from his cigarette and sighed heavily as he stared at the three graves. "I'm the last one, now," he mused. "Funny, I thought Bruce would outlive me by twenty years. He was the one who loved life."

"And you don't?" she asked, lifting her eyes.

"You work yourself to death trying to make a living, and then you die. In between, you worry about floods, droughts, taxes and capital outlay. That's about it."

"I've never known a man more cynical than you," she told him. "Not even in New York."

"I'm a realist," he corrected. "I don't expect miracles."

"Maybe that's why none ever happen for you," she said. She leaned on the cane a little and stared down at Bruce's grave. "Bruce was a dreamer. He was always looking for surprises, for the unexpected. He was a happy man most of the time, except when he remembered that he was always going to be second best. You're a hard act to follow. He never felt that he could measure up to you. He said that even your mother talked about you more than she did about him."

He raised an eyebrow. "I didn't know that. She seemed to hold me in contempt most of the time. We never understood each other."

Her quiet eyes searched his face, the hard lines around his mouth. The iron man, she mused. "I don't think anyone will ever understand you," she said quietly. "You give nothing of yourself."

His jaw tautened and his pale eyes kindled through the cloud of smoke that left his pursed lips. "Now that's an interesting statement, coming from you."

It was the emphasis he put on it. She saw with sudden clarity a picture of herself lying in his arms by the firelight, moaning as he touched her breasts....

"I didn't mean...that kind of giving," she said uneasily, and dropped her eyes to his broad chest. It strained against the denim, rippling muscles and thick dark hair that covered him from his collarbone down.

He took another draw from the cigarette. "You said before that you never had anything going with Bruce. Was that true?"

"Yes," she said simply. She searched his pale eyes. "I'm sorry there were hard feelings between you because of me. I didn't volunteer anything, you know, but he asked a lot of questions, and I was pretty upset. I don't even remember what I said to him. But I didn't tell him about...what happened. He guessed.

Maybe I looked like a fallen woman or something."
She laughed bitterly.

"You aren't a fallen woman," he said. "I came up
on your blind side, that's all. I should have realized
when you didn't put up a fight that you were too naive
to know what was happening. You thought I'd stop
in time."

She shook her head. "I trusted you, it's true. But
you didn't rape me. It was never that."

He sighed heavily and reached out a tentative hand
to brush at the loose hair around her collar, pushing
it away from her throat, from the scar on her cheek.
She shivered a little at letting him see.

"Was it very painful?" he asked tenderly.

Her lips trembled as she formed words, and around
them the wind blew cold and the sun gave barely any
warmth, and death was in the trees as well as the
graveyard.

"Yes," she whispered. She turned away, trying not
to let the feelings overwhelm her a second time. All
she seemed to do lately was cry. Impatiently, she
brushed away her tears.

Ty shifted awkwardly. He wasn't used to women
crying. He wasn't used to women, period. He didn't
know how to handle this situation.

She straightened. "I'm embarrassing you," she
murmured.

He'd forgotten how honest she was; she never
pulled her punches. Just like himself. His broad shoul-

ders rose and fell. "I'm not used to women," he told her.

She searched his eyes. "Why did Bruce tell me you were a womanizer?"

"Don't you know?" he asked quietly.

"You weren't, though, were you?" she persisted.

He reached for another cigarette and lit it. "What a hell of a question," he said shortly.

"Never mind, don't answer me; I don't care," she shot back. She moved away from the grave, putting more weight on the cane than was necessary in her anger and frustration. "I ought to go back to New York and let Ward Jessup move in with you!"

"We'd never get on," he said imperturbably, falling into step beside her. "He's a nonsmoker."

She didn't believe she'd actually heard him right. Dry humor—from Tyson Wade? She kept walking. "Bruce had moved out, hadn't he?"

"Bruce is dead," he said shortly, stopping to stare down at her. "What he did or didn't do, or said or didn't say, has nothing more to do with either of us."

"I'm sorry he's gone."

"So am I. But all the mourning in the world won't bring him back." He stared back at the grave, and for an instant there was a deep, dark hurt in his eyes. Then he erased it and turned a bland face back to Erin. "Right now, you're my top priority. I'm going to get you back on your feet again."

"I won't let you take over my life," she told him.

"Sure you will," he replied drily. "You're nothing but a little walking raincloud right now. You don't have enough spunk to fight me."

"Want to bet?" she said angrily.

"I don't gamble. Look out, you'll break that cane if you aren't careful."

"Then you'd just have to carry me home, wouldn't you?" she taunted. All the same, she lightened up on the cane. "How long do I have to stay here?"

"Until you turn sixty-five, if I know Jessup." He sighed. He glanced at her as they walked. "Put a little more weight on that leg, honey, you need to exercise it."

"Listen, cowboy...!" she snapped.

"I'm not a boy," he said.

"Will you listen to me?"

"Sure. When you say something I want to hear. Get in. I've got work to do. Winter isn't quite as hectic as the rest of the year, but I keep busy. I hope you like reading. You'll die of boredom without something to keep your mind occupied."

"I can watch television," she muttered as he helped her into the car and got in beside her.

"I don't own a television," he told her.

Her jaw fell open.

"I don't like television," he persisted, starting the car.

"What do you do in the evenings?" she asked.

"I read."

She rested her head against the seat. What a wonderful time she was going to have. In between pain pills and being forced to exercise her leg, she could sit and watch him read books. It looked as if Staghorn was going to be a great rest camp—the next best place to hell. Oh, Bruce! she thought miserably, mourning quietly for her old friend, why did you have to die and leave me in this awful mess?

Four

Erin had vowed that she wouldn't go to the doctor, but Ty simply put her in the car and drove her there. To make matters worse, he raised eyebrows in the crowded waiting room by insisting on going in with her to talk to the doctor.

Her face flushed wildly as they followed the nurse down the hall.

"This will be all over town in no time," she groaned. "How could you do that to me?"

"Everybody knows you're living out at the ranch anyway," he said reasonably.

He was right, but that didn't make her feel any more comfortable about it. She hated being the object of idle gossip. People probably already knew that she was getting half of Staghorn, and she could just imagine what they figured she'd done to earn it.

"Will you stop torturing yourself?" he grumbled, glancing down at her as they stepped into the examination room. "What the hell does it matter if people talk?"

"Well, it won't be your reputation that gets ruined, will it?" she returned.

"Miss Scott? I'm Dr. Alex Brodie." The elderly, white-coated man entered right behind them and shook hands with Erin and then with Ty. He sat down and went over the details of her surgery with her. Apparently Ty had given him her doctor's name and he'd had a conversation with the man, because he knew exactly what had been done as well as the exercises that had been prescribed.

"Have you been doing the physical therapy?" he asked.

She colored delicately and averted her eyes. "There didn't seem much point," she began.

"Miss Scott, may I be blunt?" he asked, and proceeded to be so. "Surgery can help only to a certain point. You can walk again, but unless you do the exercises, exactly as prescribed, that leg will be stiff for the rest of your life, and you'll always limp. I understand that you were a professional model. That makes it even more important for you to exercise—

if, that is, you have any idea of going back to work in the future.''

She stared at her hands, clenched in her lap. How could Ty do this to her?

"We can, of course, have you drive to the hospital each day, and a physical therapist can instruct you and work with you.''

She looked up, her eyes disturbed. ''Oh, no. Please,'' she asked gently. ''I couldn't bear that....''

"Suppose I work with her at the ranch,'' Ty suggested. He was sitting cross-legged in a chair, hat on one knee, looking impossibly arrogant. ''I had a busted hip once, remember?''

The doctor cleared his throat. ''Oh, how I remember!'' he said. ''One of my best nurses quit, two physical therapists retired...''

Ty just grinned, and Erin gaped at him, unbelieving. She'd hardly ever seen him smile like that.

"I could give you a list of the exercises,'' the doctor murmured. ''But she'll have to do them twice a day, every day, thirty minutes at a stretch.''

"She'll do them,'' Ty promised before Erin could open her mouth.

"I'd like to examine that hip now,'' he added, calling his nurse into the room.

Erin glared at Ty. ''Unless you're planning to do a consultation, *Dr.* Wade, would you mind leaving?''

He cocked an eyebrow as he rose. ''Testy little

thing, aren't you?" He moved past her. "Watch out," he told the doctor. "She bites."

"Be sure your tetanus jabs are current," she whispered as he left the room.

It was amazing, the ease of that repartee, when once she'd been too tongue-tied to talk to him. In spite of everything that had happened between them, she was still drawn to him. Ty was stronger than any other human being she'd ever known. Just for a little while, she needed to lean on someone. And who better than the man who was partially responsible for her condition?

Dr. Brodie looked at the stitches, had an X ray made, and pronounced her well on the way to recovery. He prescribed some additional pain pills, in case she needed them, and gave her a preprinted sheet of exercises with special ones circled.

She stared at them all the way back to Staghorn, dreading the ordeal they represented.

"I don't want to start this," she muttered. "All that pain and cramping, and for what? I'll always limp!"

"Not if you want to walk," he returned impassively. "But you have to be willing to do the work. I'll help, but I can't do it for you."

"Why should you want to help?" she asked, turning in the seat to fix him with a cold, level stare.

He was smoking. He took a draw from the cigarette before he answered, and he didn't look at her. "Because I did that to you, as surely as if I'd pushed you in front of another car.''

She stared at him uncomprehendingly. ''Surely you don't think that you caused me to have the wreck?''

''Didn't I?'' He laughed mirthlessly. ''You were half hysterical when you left here.''

''Yes, I was. And I pulled off the road and got myself together before I ever left the ranch!'' she told him. ''I'm not suicidal, and I'm not homicidal. I never drive when I'm not fit emotionally. By the time the wreck happened, I was at least levelheaded. Even the state patrol said it was unavoidable. I was hit by a drunk driver who took a curve too wide and came at me in my lane. He was killed outright.''

Ty's face paled, and his hands clenched the steering wheel tightly. ''Lucky man,'' he said under his breath. Erin knew what he meant without asking for explanations.

''So if you're on some guilt trip, let me reassure you,'' she continued quietly. ''The only thing you did was try to save your brother from me. And you succeeded.''

''Beyond my wildest dreams,'' he said coldly, lifting the cigarette to his lips. ''I ruined both your lives.''

She could hardly believe what she was hearing. He sounded bitter, anguished. ''What could you have done that would have changed anything?'' she asked calmly. "I would never have married Bruce. I didn't love him, and he knew it."

He glanced at her. "Maybe if I hadn't made a dead set at you, he'd have had a chance."

She shook her head firmly. "Not that way."

His eyes held hers for an instant before they returned to the road. "Didn't you ever want him?"

"Not physically. He was good fun; a nice, undemanding companion. I didn't want affairs, like some of the girls did. The fact that he had money never made him any more special to me. I like making my own way." She leaned her head against the seat and studied his uneven features quietly. "At least you never suspected me of being a gold-digger."

"I knew better," he said with a faint smile. "I tried to buy you off at first, if you remember. You took the check straight to Bruce and handed it to him in front of me. That cured me."

"And surprised you, I guess."

He nodded. "I'd thought I had you pegged. And I never really knew you at all." He turned onto the long ranch road that led back to Staghorn, down a driveway that boasted rough wood fenceposts, electrified fencing and mesquite groves everywhere among bare, leafless trees. "I thought you'd been to bed with half-a-dozen men. I got the shock of my life that night."

She felt her face growing warm. They shared such intimate memories, for two old enemies.

"Erin, why did you give in to me?" he asked unexpectedly. "You must have suspected what I was doing."

She looked at him, admiring the play of muscles in his arms as he manipulated the car along the dirt road. "Yes," she replied after a moment. "I suspected it."

"Then why give in? Were you really so trusting that you didn't realize what I had in mind?"

"I was too far gone to care," she said quietly, avoiding his suddenly piercing gaze. "I'd never felt like that with a man. I didn't want you to stop. By the time I was fully aware of what I was doing, it was much too late to say no."

"I would have stopped if you'd asked me, all the same," he said, jerking the wheel as he turned up toward the house.

"You couldn't have."

He pulled up at the front steps and turned to her. "I could have," he said firmly. "I wasn't that far gone until the last few seconds."

Her face went beet red as he looked at her, because she remembered those last few seconds with shocking clarity.

"You pulled me down to you," he said in a tone that was husky and deep, and unfamiliar. "I knew that your body was rejecting me, and why, and I was just starting to pull back. And you reached up to my hips and dug those long, exquisite nails into me, and I was lost."

Her breath caught in her throat. She tried to reply and failed, and he touched her lips with the very tip of his finger, probing them delicately apart so he could see the pearly whiteness of her teeth.

"I didn't even give you pleasure," he continued roughly. "I took you, used you, and you should have hated me for it. But you didn't. Your eyes were like velvet—so soft that I got lost in them. And I wanted to do it again, to try and make it right. But I started thinking about Bruce, and some things he'd said...and I was afraid to trust you. So I fed you a lot of bull about ruining you with Bruce and ran you off."

Her eyes widened, darkened. "You...really wanted me, didn't you?" she asked gently.

"Until you were an obsession," he replied, his voice low and slightly harsh. "You were so beautiful, Erin. Any man would have died to have you."

Then, perhaps, she thought. But not now, not with her scars and her limp and her lack of confidence. She averted her eyes. "Those days are over now," she said dully. "I'm not the same person."

"Aren't you? You could be, if you wanted to."

"With my scars?" Her voice broke, and she jerked away from him, wounded. Her eyes sparked at his puzzled face. "You wanted me when I was beautiful; you wanted me because Bruce did. But now I'm crippled and hurt, and you feel sorry for me. That's the only reason you're even tolerating me, Ty! You were my enemy from the first day we met. Even then, you looked at me as if you hated me!''

Of course he had, he mused, searching her cold face. He'd wanted her. Needed her. It had all been a defense against being hurt himself. He'd fought her because he wanted her so much, and he knew in his heart that she'd never want someone like him. But he couldn't tell her that. He couldn't let her know how vulnerable he'd been.

''So you're crippled,'' he said easily, brutally. ''And apparently you like being that way, and feeling sorry for yourself, because you're not making any effort to change it. I guess you want to live under my roof and depend on me for every crumb you eat for the rest of your life, is that right?''

It was a calculated risk—it might send her into spasms of weeping, for which he'd hate himself. But he was betting it would have the opposite effect.

It did. Her eyes began to blaze. Her face went white with pent-up fury. She swung at him immediately, and he caught her wrist with her hand just a fraction of an inch from his jaw.

He jerked, pulling her across the wide seat and into his hard arms, and held her against him relentlessly.

''You…!'' She struggled frantically until her own sharp movements brought pain. Then she stiffened, feeling the knifelike stab in her hip, and gasped.

''See what you get?'' he chided. He held her with one arm while his lean hand massaged the throbbing hip through the thick corduroy of her dark slacks. "Does that help?"

"Stop it," she muttered, spitting out a strand of hair that had worked its way between her lips. "Oh, I do hate you, Tyson Radley Wade!"

His pale eyes kindled. "I didn't know you knew my middle name."

She shifted, grimacing as his kneading freed the tense muscles from their cramp. "I saw...your birth certificate...with Bruce's when we were looking at the family album one night."

His hand was less therapeutic now than blatantly caressing. He moved it slowly over her hip, watching her face curiously. "Odd that you'd remember something like that, seeing how much you hate me," he murmured.

"Ty..."

"That's how you said my name," he breathed, bending, "when I touched you for the first time. You moaned it, just like that, and the blood rushed into my head like fire."

"I didn't...moan it," she whispered. His mouth was almost against hers, and she stared at its hard, thin curve as if hypnotized. She didn't want him to kiss her. It was too soon; there had been too much pain....

But he was already doing it. His hard mouth caught hers roughly and took it, possessed it. He groaned, jerking her breasts close against his chest, crushing her mouth feverishly under the hardness of his.

She pushed against him, feeling the steely warmth of his muscular chest through his shirt, the powerful beat of his heart beneath her fingers. He wasn't giving her room to respond, even if she'd been able to. He was taking. Just taking.

At last, her lack of response seemed to get through to him. He lifted his mouth and stared into her eyes.

"What am I doing wrong?" he whispered huskily. "Show me."

She wondered at his choice of words, but only for a moment. It had been months, and the feel of him was making her weak. She reached up without thinking, curving her slender fingers against his cheek, and pulled him closer. She nibbled at his mouth, her lips barely touching his, probing gently, brushing so that he could feel their very texture.

"Like this?" he murmured, and followed her lead.

The soft brushing movements of his warm mouth made her tingle. She smiled against his lips and moved her breasts gently over his chest so that he could feel them. He stiffened, and his arms contracted with bruising force.

"Ty!" she whispered reprovingly. "Not so hard, please!"

He was breathing roughly. He let her move away, watching her hand go to her sore breasts, and his eyes traced them curiously. "You're delicate there," he said. "I didn't think. Did I hurt them?" He moved his hand over hers, lightly touching her, as if a woman's body were a new and mysterious phenomenon.

"I'm all right," she said breathlessly.

His fingers eased between hers, so that they were warm on the curve of her breast. His eyes locked with hers, and she could see the pupils dilating.

His lips parted as he found the hard tip of her breast with one long finger and began to rub it gently through the fabric of her blouse. She jerked helplessly and gasped, and he did it a little harder. He watched her bite her lip and realized that she was biting back a moan, because her expression was one of pleasure, not pain.

"God, that excites me," he breathed roughly. "Watching you like this drives me crazy!"

She could feel that; he'd turned her so that her belly was lying against his, and she knew that he was fully aroused.

He nuzzled his cheek against hers, hiding his glittering eyes. His hand gently moved hers aside and covered her breast, savoring its soft firmness, tracing its contours as if he'd never touched a woman like that before.

She was scarcely breathing at all, the pain forgotten, the memories forgotten. There was only *now*, and the silence of the closed car, the rasp of Ty's breathing at her ear, the furious throbbing of his heart.

There was the sound of his hand smoothing the cotton print of her blouse, the whispery gasps she couldn't stifle, and the feel of his hard arms as she gripped him for support.

He kissed her cheek, her ear, his lips tender, urgent. His hand fumbled with buttons, and he muttered something under his breath as he found her bra and couldn't figure out how to get it open. Finally, he settled for sliding his hand roughly underneath, lifting her free of the lacy cup, and he groaned again as he felt the softness fill his hand, felt the hardness grinding into his damp palm.

"Ty..." Her voice sounded oddly high-pitched, helpless. She turned in his arms and buried her face in his chest, clinging to him.

He went over the edge at the unexpected vulnerability. He nuzzled her cheek with his lips; then, finding her mouth, he kissed it hungrily with a rough kind of tenderness. His hand cupped her breast warmly, insistently, and it was a long time before he lifted his head and looked down.

His skin was dark against hers, dark against the telltale paleness of flesh shielded from the harsh light of the sun. And the sight of his hand there, possessing her, made her flush feverishly.

He caught her eyes. "Have you had anyone since me?" he whispered huskily.

"No," she replied honestly.

"I haven't had anyone since you." His eyes traveled down to the softness in his hand. "Oh, God, Erin, you're so beautiful."

Her lips parted on a rush of exhaled breath. What was she letting him do? Where was her pride? He hadn't caused the wreck, but if he'd listened to her, it might have been prevented. She'd lost her baby, she was crippled....

She pulled away from him, crumpling her blouse together as she avoided his eyes. She was breathing hard, but so was he.

"I guess I shouldn't have done that," he said hesitantly.

"I shouldn't have let you," she had the grace to admit.

He took a steadying breath and removed his dress Stetson to smooth his damp hair. "We'd better go inside," he said, aware of his surroundings for the first time. He was grateful that it was José and Conchita's afternoon off, and that the hands were all busy in the equipment barn. Thank God for tinted windows and large shade trees and the privacy of a big car. He straightened, feeling sore all over from frustrated desire. He could hardly believe that she'd given him such license, after all that had happened. Perhaps, he thought, there was a little hope left.

"Are you all right?" she asked softly.

He stared at her, his face hard but his eyes kindling with a new emotion. "I just hurt a little," he said honestly. "Nothing to bother about. How's your hip?"

She swallowed. "I...uh...hadn't noticed." She touched it gingerly. "I don't enjoy being a cripple," she added, belatedly remembering the source of the argument. "And I'll be glad to do the exercises if it will convince you that I don't want to 'live off you.'"

"Good," he said with the hint of a smile. "I don't want to live off you, either. So suppose we start those exercises tonight? I think I could learn to like massaging that hip for you."

"You weren't massaging it."

"What was I doing, then?" he asked innocently.

She glared at him and got out of the car. And was so flustered that she walked firmly on her damaged side for the first time since the surgery.

Five

That was the first night Ty didn't withdraw into his study immediately after supper to work on his books. He had all kinds of equipment in there, including a state of the art computer with a vast memory in which he kept records of all his cattle. It was, Erin later learned, only a terminal, which was connected to the mainframe in his office. And he had two offices: one on the ranch itself, and another that he shared with several partners in some sweeping cattle-investment corporation. He had his finger in several pies—which accounted for his wealth.

"It takes a lot of figuring to keep up with it all," he told her as they went into the living room for their after-dinner coffee. "I have accountants, but I don't trust my books completely to anyone. I've seen outfits ruined just because the man on top didn't want to be bothered with paperwork and made his people second-guess what he wanted done."

"You don't really trust anyone, do you?" she asked, curious. She sat down in a big armchair across from the sofa, careful not to look toward the fireplace. This was the room where Ty had seduced her, and the memories were disturbing.

"Oh, I don't know," he murmured, watching her. "I guess I'm learning to trust you a little."

"You didn't have much choice, with Bruce's will left the way it was," she replied. She toyed with the skirt of her pale-green jersey dress. "I guess you were pretty upset when you found out what he'd done."

"Ward Jessup and I go back a long way," he said dryly. "I wouldn't have jumped for joy at the prospect of oil rigs mingling with my purebred Santa Gertrudis."

"I imagine not." She looked up. "But how did you know I wouldn't deliberately stay away just to make sure that happened?"

"I didn't," he confessed. He lit a cigarette and leaned back, his dark slacks and light shirt straining against the powerful muscles of an utterly masculine body. His hair was immaculately groomed, thick and black and straight, his face clean-shaven. He always looked neat, even when he was working cattle. Despite his lack of conventional good looks, he was more of a man than anyone Erin had ever known.

"I thought about it," she admitted with a faint smile. "And then I thought about how many people would be out of work because of my stiff pride."

"Softhearted liberal," he chided gently. "Wouldn't it have been worth it to see me brought to my knees after what I did to you?"

Her eyes searched his, and she felt the electricity that had never completely faded between them. "All I really could blame you for was listening to Bruce's lies and refusing to listen to me."

"Think so?" He got up and poured himself a brandy. She noticed that he didn't offer her one and remembered that she'd always refused liquor in the past. He didn't forget much.

"Anyway, it's over and done now," she murmured.

He turned, the brandy glass in one lean hand, staring at her intently. "Do you think it's that easy for me?"

She stared at him, bewildered. "I don't understand."

"You were carrying my child," he said in a tone that went straight to her heart. He looked down into the brandy snifter, sloshing the liquid around as if its color fascinated him. "You can't imagine how I felt when I read that letter, when I knew what I'd done."

Somehow breath had suspended itself in her throat.

She felt as if she were drowning in the depths of his pale eyes, held there by something new and strange and vulnerable. He'd always seemed incapable of emotion, yet for one moment, one heart-stopping eternity, his expression had held such pain—such agonized loss—that now she was powerless to move, to speak, even to think.

He lifted his head and stared at the painting above the mantel. It was a scene of Texas that had been done by someone in his family almost a century ago, of longhorn cattle in a storm with a ranch house and windmill in the background.

"Erin..." He paused as if searching for words, his back straight and rigid. "I didn't plan what happened that night. I told you I had, but it wasn't the truth...."

Her hands fiddled with her skirt as she stared at him in wonder. He'd never talked to her like this. She waited silently for him to continue.

"I thought if I goaded you, I might make you mad enough to strike out at me," he said, lifting his eyes to the painting. "When you did, it gave me an excuse to touch you. I'd wanted that. You obsessed me, haunted me. I dreamed about how it would be, touching you that way." He shrugged wearily. "You kissed me back, and I went crazy. To this day, I don't half remember how it happened. I didn't even think about taking precautions. I assumed that you were already doing it, that you were experienced."

The confession fascinated her. She studied the hard

muscles of his legs, his narrow hips, remembering how they'd felt under her exploring hands. She flushed a little at the memory. "I thought it was to get me out of Bruce's life."

He turned, pinning her with quiet, steady eyes. "I lied," he said. "Bruce was the last thing on my mind. I wanted you."

She felt like a trapped animal. He was doing it again, trying to take her over, own her. She clenched her hands tightly in her lap. "You let me go," she whispered.

"I had to, damn it!" he cried. "You were his, for all practical purposes. I'd betrayed him; so had you. I couldn't live with it. I had to get you out of here before I..."

"Before what, iron man?" she asked him. "Before you lost your head again? Is it so hard to admit that you're human enough to feel desire?"

"Yes!"

He slammed the brandy snifter into the fire, watching it splinter amid the explosion of blazing liquor. Erin jumped at the impact, but he didn't even flinch. He brushed back a lock of unruly hair and reached automatically into his pocket for a cigarette. He lit it and took a long draw while Erin sat nervously watching him.

He moved away from the fireplace restlessly. "My father's idea of marriage was warped. He saw it as a business merger. Sex, he always told me, was a weakness that a man with any backbone should be able to overcome." He paused in front of her and looked down, his silvery eyes cold and unfeeling. "Erin, I had my first woman when I was twenty-one, and it took weeks to get over the guilt. I gave in to a desire I couldn't control, and I hated it. And her." He lifted his shoulders. "Maybe I hated my father, too, for forcing his principles onto me. My mother couldn't live with him. She was normal. A warm, loving woman. He couldn't even touch her at the last."

He moved back to the fireplace and stared into the flames while Erin sat quietly and thrilled to the wonder of hearing these intimate things—things, she knew, that he'd never shared with another living soul.

"I'm more like him every day," he said dully, studying the flames. "I can't change. Walls work both ways. They keep people out...but they keep people in, too."

Her heart ached for him. Her own problems seemed to diminish a little as she realized what he was saying.

"You're lonely," she said gently.

He turned and looked at her, and for the first time his expression wasn't hidden. He seemed older, worn; and there was pain in every line of his hard face. "Honey, I've been lonely all my life," he said, his voice deep and quiet, the endearment curiously exciting to Erin because it was so unlike him. "My upbringing and my looks have been two strikes against me with women ever since I can remember."

She blinked. "Your looks?"

"Don't be coy," he muttered. "I know I'm no prize."

"If you think looks make any difference, you're no prize mentally, and that's for sure," she said slowly, deliberately. "I've never known anyone who was more a man than you are."

His eyes widened, as if the compliment had shocked him. He stared at her, the cigarette forgotten. "I hurt you...."

"I was a virgin," she said softly. "Sometimes it's difficult for women the first time. You couldn't have helped that."

His jaw tensed. "Coals of fire, Erin."

She remembered the quotation from the Bible, about heaping coals of fire on an enemy's head by being kind to him. "It isn't flattery," she told him. "I don't like you enough to flatter you."

He actually laughed. "Aiding and abetting the enemy, then?"

She shrugged. "The enemy's managed to bring me back to life. I think I owe you a compliment or two."

"You won't think so when I start on that hip," he assured her. He lifted his chin imperiously and smiled. "Drill instructors will look like pussycats when I get through with you."

"You were a marine, weren't you?" she shot back. "'Once a marine, always a marine'—isn't that what they say? Well, you won't break me, mister. I'm tough!''

He liked her spirit. He always had. But the woman he'd found in that New York apartment hadn't shown any. It had taken this trip and a lot of goading, but he'd managed to shake her out of all that self-pitying apathy. And he was pleased with the result.

"You're pretty like that," he remarked, noting the color in her cheeks, the emerald depths of her eyes, the provocative disorder of all that black hair curling around her elfin face. "Scars and all. In no time at all, you'll never know where the cuts were."

"My hip will never look the same without skin grafts," she muttered, brought back to painful reality. "And I don't really want to go through any more surgery."

"Once a man got you undressed, a scar on your hip would be the last thing he'd be staring at," he said bluntly.

She'd forgotten that he'd seen her by the firelight without her clothing. She remembered that frank appraisal, as if he'd never seen a nude woman before and wanted to memorize every soft line and curve. Her breasts had fascinated him. He'd touched them so gently, caressed them, whispered how beautiful they were. Without warning, her face went scarlet.

"Yes, you remember too, don't you?" he asked, his voice low and sensuous. "It was right where I'm standing, and I looked at you until I got drunk on the sight. And you let me. You lay there all soft and sweetly moving, and you let me.''

"It was new," she said defensively, lowering her eyes to her dress.

"It was heaven," he corrected. "The closest I ever expect to get in my lifetime. If it hadn't been for Bruce..." He turned and threw his cigarette into the fire, closing his eyes against the pain. "Oh, God, I'll never forgive him!"

His tone of voice disturbed her. It was bitter, yet filled with the anguish of loss...profound loss. She got up, unconsciously walking without the cane, limping a little as she paused beside him.

He was so tall. Towering. She had to look up to see his dark face, and the warmth and strength of him drew her like a magnet. It had been so sweet that afternoon to lie in his arms again and feel his mouth; and those memories were her undoing.

"It doesn't matter anymore," she said gently. "He's dead. Let him rest in peace. He had so little of it in life, Ty."

"How much do you think I have?" he demanded, staring down at her with tormented eyes. "It's eating me alive!"

She held him by the arms and actually shook him. "The car came at me around a curve, head on," she said, frustrated into telling him the truth about the wreck. "Nobody could have avoided it, upset or not!"

He watched her without speaking for a long moment. "Is that the truth?"

"Yes! And it was in New York State, just minutes from home, Ty. I could have been driving out of the city to an assignment and had it happen." She held his eyes with her own, adding slowly, "You didn't cause it."

He shook his head and smiled grimly. "Didn't I?" He took a slow breath and seemed to notice her hands for the first time. "Would you have had the baby?"

"Of course," she said without thinking.

He reached out and touched her cheek where the hairline scar ran just beside her ear. "Someone would have told me, eventually," he said quietly. "I'd have come to you. I'd have married you."

"What kind of life would that have been?" she asked sadly, searching the hard lines of his face. "You'd never have accepted what I did for a living, or even the way I was. You didn't want a butterfly— you even said so. And modeling was my whole life. I loved it; I loved the bright lights and the people and the delight of showing off pretty clothes." The smile that had animated her face faded as she remembered the wreck. "I lost all that. I can't go back to it, not like this. I can learn another kind of work, but nothing will ever replace modeling." *Except you,* she wanted to say. But she couldn't. She couldn't lower her pride enough to tell him that living with him and being loved by him would have been more than enough recompense for the career she'd lost.

She turned back toward the sofa, stumbling a little.

"Oh, damn this leg!" she burst out, near tears.

"If you don't like it, suppose you fix it," he said. "Exercise it, like the doctor told you. If you want your career back, earn it!"

She couldn't know that her remark about her career had caught him on the raw, that he was hurting because she'd as much as told him that he didn't matter. He deserved it, he knew he did, but it cut all the same.

"Okay," she told him defiantly. "I will!"

He smiled. "Good. Now go get on something you can exercise in and I'll coach you. We can have coffee later."

She hobbled down the hall to her room without a backward glance. And she told herself she hated him more than ever.

The first session was more painful than she'd anticipated. She did the exercises described on the sheet, with Ty looming over her, demanding more than she thought she was capable of.

"You can push harder than that, for God's sake," he said when she slackened.

"I'm not a man!"

He looked pointedly at her firm, full breasts under the revealing fabric of her body leotard, and a faint smile touched his mouth. "I'll drink to that."

"Stop looking at me there," she told him haughtily.

"Wear a bra next time," he countered, watching her from his armchair as she stretched on the carpet. "I can't help it if I get disturbed by hard nipples."

She gasped, flushed, and sat up in one sharp movement. "Tyson!" she burst out.

His eyebrows arched, and he looked as hopelessly the dominant male as any movie sex symbol. "Why the red-rose blush, honey?" he asked innocently. "Or don't you remember that you had sex with me on this very carpet?"

"Oh, I hate you!" she cried, eyes flaring, cheeks flaming, hair disordered and wild around her oval face. The leotard emphasized her thinness, but it also lovingly outlined a body so exquisite that lingerie companies had bid for her services as a model.

"No you don't; you just hate sex," he replied. "And that's my fault. But one of these days, I may change your mind about that."

"Hold your breath," she challenged.

"Daring me, Erin?" he asked, and his smile held shades of meaning as his silver eyes glittered over her body.

Watching those eyes, she began to tingle from head to toe. Her hip was throbbing, but she felt reckless all the same. She wanted to wipe that arrogant smile off his face. She wanted to make him vulnerable, wanted to watch the walls come down.

She arched her back, just a little, just enough to make the hard tips of her breasts blatantly visible. "Maybe I am," she whispered huskily. "So what are you going to do about it, cattle king?"

He was smoking a cigarette, but at her words he deliberately crushed it out in the ashtray. "I hope your hip's up to some additional exercise," he drawled.

And with a movement so fast it blurred, he slid down over her body and pinned her there, arching above her with one lean, muscular leg thrown heavily over both of hers.

"Okay, honey, now what do we do?" he said softly. "Is this what you had in mind?" And looking down, he blatantly slid one lean hand directly over a full breast, cupping it.

She felt her breath catch. Watching him earlier— and now—a lot of things were becoming clear to her. The way he'd been in the car, hungry but not practised; the way he was cupping her now, blatantly, without any preliminaries: she had a deep hunch that he knew less about women than he was pretending to. Male pride obviously ran deep. Well, two could play at this game. She didn't know a lot, either, but she'd heard women talk....

"Not like that," she whispered, lifting his hand. "Like...this."

She showed him how to trace the softness, to tease the tip until her body stiffened and trembled with the need to be touched. She drew his fingers against her until he understood and began to do it without coaching.

"You like it that way?" he asked under his breath, searching her eyes for an instant before they went back to the softness of her body under his hand.

"Yes," she whispered shakily. "It arouses me."

His breath shuddered out of him. He could hardly believe it, that she was willing to show him what she liked, that she wasn't complaining about his lack of finesse or laughing at him. All at once he wondered if Bruce had been lying after all, about that. She didn't seem the kind of woman to laugh at inexperience… especially now.

"What else do you like?" he asked huskily.

It was like drinking wine. She felt drunk on him. Her hip was forgotten, every other thought drained away. She was woman enticing man. She was a siren trapping a sailor, giddy with her own power.

Her hands eased up to the shoulders of the leotard, and, holding his fascinated gaze, she drew it down and bared her taut breasts.

"Oh, God…" He shuddered as he saw their creamy fullness, the dark mauve points lifting gracefully toward him. "Oh, God, you're beautiful, baby…!"

She felt beautiful. She felt achingly hungry as well. She reached up with trembling hands to take his hard face and draw it toward her body.

"What do you want?" he whispered, frowning.

"I want you to put your lips...here." She touched her breasts lightly, caressing their swollen peaks.

He stopped breathing. "On your breasts?" he asked hesitantly. "I won't hurt them?"

She felt the smile in her eyes as she shook her head. "Oh, no," she promised. "You won't hurt them."

He eased his hands under her bare back to lift her, bending over her in spite of his reservations. But her body had a scent like roses, and when he touched his mouth to the curve of her soft breast, she stiffened and began to tremble like a rain-tossed leaf.

More confident now, he began to draw his lips around the very tip of her breast. And when that made her moan softly, he opened his mouth and took the nipple inside, warming it with his tongue. She cried out then, and just as he thought he'd hurt her and tried to move away, her hands dug into the nape of his neck and she arched her soft body up to him with a tiny whimpered plea.

He groaned himself at the surge of pleasure it gave him to know that she was enjoying it, too. His hands smoothed down her rib cage, savoring her warm, silky skin while his mouth fed on the unexpected sweetness of her breasts.

When he lifted his head, her expression shocked and delighted him. Her eyes were half closed, watching him, her lips parted over pearly teeth. Her face was alive with color, her hands caressing the hard muscle of his chest.

"Could you take off your shirt?" she asked drowsily.

He couldn't take it off fast enough, in fact. His hands fumbled because he was aroused—as he hadn't been since that night with her. But that night was nothing like this. He was on fire. Burning up.

He ripped off the shirt and shuddered a little with pride as her eyes ran over him with blatant appreciation. She reached up hesitantly, smoothing over the thick mat of hair that covered the warm, bronzed muscles, and at her touch he felt his heart running wild.

She lifted herself up gracefully and kneeled in front of him. Her eyes traced his torso, and she seemed to sway toward him. She dug her nails into his muscular arms and leaned a little against him, drawing the very tips of her breasts softly, abrasively, against the hardness of his chest.

He shuddered violently. "Erin!" he gasped.

"Oh, Ty..." It was as much a moan as a whisper. She put her mouth on his and kissed him hungrily, feeling his arms come around her, crushing her, trembling as they fit her exquisitely to the contours of his chest. The hair was cushy and thick, and she liked the feel of it against her soft breasts. She could feel his heartbeat shaking both of them. It was so sweet. So sweet...

The sudden intrusion of a knock on the front door

made her almost sick with mingled frustration and shock.

She jerked back. He looked as dazed as she felt. He looked at her one last time and cursed under his breath as he helped her back into the leotard.

He got to his feet gracefully and was just shouldering into his shirt when they heard footsteps echoing down the hall. Erin looked toward the door—and realized they'd both forgotten to close it!

"I used to be levelheaded before you came along," Ty muttered, glaring at her as he fastened buttons. "My God, with the door standing wide open...! You little siren," he breathed, his eyes warm with memories as they held hers. "God, that was sweet!"

"Well, you're helping me get back on my feet," she murmured demurely. "I thought the least I could do was divert you a little."

"That was more seduction than diversion," he replied. He reached down a hand to help her up. But instead of letting her go, he held her just in front of him. "Erin, we've got to do something about this," he said solemnly. "You knock me off balance pretty bad. I could lose control, now more than ever. I...don't want to make you pregnant by accident." The thought seemed to torture him; his face hardened into grim lines, his eyes grew dark.

"I'm sorry," Erin said quietly. "I won't do it again. I don't know what got into me, Ty..."

"No," he whispered, touching her mouth with his

forefinger. "No, don't apologize for it. You made me feel like a man again, like a whole man...." He hesitated uncharacteristically. "I want you." He said it in a whisper, as if it were some terrible secret.

She drew in a slow breath. "I know." She dropped her eyes to his chest. She could have said the same thing, but she was afraid to give him that kind of power over her. His hands gripped her arms painfully hard just as José came to the door.

"*Señor*, it is the foreman, Señor Grandy. A wild dog has brought down a calf. He says it is the same dog as before, that of Señor Jessup."

"Damn," Ty muttered. Instantly he was the powerful cattle baron again, cold, relentless, indomitable; a formidable adversary. And a stranger. "Get my .30-.30 and bring me a box of ammunition," he ordered José. "And tell Grandy to wait for me. Call Ed Johnson while I'm gone and tell him the situation. I may have a court suit over this."

"*Sí, señor,*" José said graciously, and left them.

"It's Mr. Jessup's dog?" she asked Ty, watching him reach into the closet for his sheepskin jacket and the familiar old Stetson he wore when he was working.

"That's about the size of it. Part shepherd, part wolf. I've told him about that dog, but he won't pen it up. I've lost my last calf to it."

"But what if he sues you?" she asked.

"Let him. I like a good fight." He buttoned the

coat and studied her in the tight leotard. "Get a good night's sleep. Tomorrow, you and I have to talk."

He came close then, framing her face in his lean hands. "I may be late. Don't wait up."

He bent and put his mouth softly against hers, with a new tenderness. She smiled against his lips and bit at the lower one.

He jerked back, frowning. And then he repeated the tiny caress on her own lip, smiling slowly at the reaction.

"How do you know so much about kissing?" he murmured.

"Because up until you came along, that was all I ever did with boys," she replied, and searched his eyes. "Be careful out there."

"Worried about the enemy?" he asked mockingly.

She touched his cheek. "Who would I fight with if something happened to you?" she asked noncommittally.

He brushed his finger against her mouth, brooding. "Erin... No. I can't talk about it now. Good night."

He left her without a backward glance, taking his rifle and ammunition from José on his way through the hall. She heard the front door slam behind him, and felt chilled to the bone.

What, she wondered, had he been about to say to her?

Six

Erin felt haunted that night. She couldn't help remembering Bruce and Ty and the way things had
been. She recalled vividly one particular day, when
she and Bruce were going for a ride in the chill of
the early morning.

Ty had been working with one of his horses that
day, and he'd stopped just long enough to tell Bruce
which horse to saddle for Erin…

Bruce had bowed low, then glared up at him, all
boyish and defiant. "I do know how to pick a horse,"
he'd drawled sarcastically. "I won't let her get hurt,
either. After all," he'd added pointedly, "she is my
girl, not yours."

Ty hadn't said a word. But he'd looked at Erin, and his silver eyes had been faintly hungry, possessive. Even in memory, the intensity of his gaze made her tingle. Up until that moment, Ty had been openly hostile, taunting her at every opportunity, picking at her, mocking her. But on that cold morning, there had been something in his eyes that had excited her, attracted her.

He'd held her gaze until she'd wondered if her heart could stand it. It had been like holding a live wire in wet hands. Her lips had parted, and his narrowed eyes had gone to them hungrily. If Bruce hadn't chosen that moment to reappear with Erin's mount, anything might have happened.

She'd relived that look all through the ride. When they'd returned, Bruce had been sidetracked by one of the stable boys.

Erin had spotted Ty, standing all alone by the corral, staring into the distance. And for some reason that she still didn't completely understand, she'd run to him.

Even now, she could see the expression on his hard, homely face, shock mingling with pure pleasure as she'd come toward him, her long black hair flaring behind her, her eyes alive with the joy of living. She'd darted up onto the lowest rail of the corral fence, beside him, and talked enthusiastically about the ride and the ranch and how much she was enjoying her visit.

Surprisingly, he hadn't been sarcastic or ridiculing. He'd smoked his cigarette calmly and answered all her curious questions, even seemed to enjoy them. But there still had been that hunger in his eyes when he'd looked at her. And it hadn't been very much later that Bruce had gone out on business and Ty had made one cutting remark too many.

She could still remember the feel of his hard cheek under her flashing hand, the shocked amusement in his face as he'd reached out arrogantly and jerked her against his hard-muscled body.

She'd thrilled to the unfamiliar contact...and all the arguments had suddenly made sense as the very real, explosive passion between them had been unleashed at last.

"At last," he'd whispered roughly, bending to her mouth. "Oh, God, at last..."

She hadn't questioned that strange wording, and when his lips had come crashing down against hers, she'd forgotten everything in the magic of being touched by him. For a long time, she'd forbidden her mind to relive that ecstatic night, but now she wanted to remember. She savored again the shocked gasp that had burst from his throat as she'd reached toward him instead of pushing him away, the pulsating hardness of his body as he'd smoothed her against its every rippling muscle and deepened the warm, rough kiss.

He hadn't been experienced. She'd known he was no virgin, but in retrospect, she realized that every movement had been spontaneous, unpremeditated. He'd wanted her desperately, and she'd wanted him. The nearness of him, the warmth of his mouth, the strength of his body—she'd wanted it all, without realizing what her desire meant to an aroused man. Her experience was even less than his...so that what happened had been inevitable. Inevitable...like the wreck...

She touched her flat stomach with gentle hands and felt the sting of tears in her eyes. The hardest thing of all had been losing the baby. She remembered how she'd cried when they'd told her about the miscarriage, about her crushed pelvis. The world had gone dark with Ty's stubborn refusal to listen, with his harsh renunciation. The wreck, the miscarriage, the terrible ordeal of surgery...it had been nightmarish....

And now, because of the horror, she was here, close to Ty, beginning a relationship that was new and a little frightening. Did he only feel pity for her? And what did she feel? At first she'd wanted revenge; she'd hated him. But in time, she'd stopped being so terribly bitter and had drifted into a kind of numb apathy. Now she was back to stinging life again—and all because of Ty.

She rolled over onto her back with a troubled sigh. She felt desire; that much was sadly evident. Every time he touched her, her willpower vanished. She was his. And he had to know that. But he seemed hesitant, too.

His father had warped him, she realized. His ideas of intimacy and marriage were distorted. He didn't seem to know a great deal about women or closeness or giving. There was still a side of him that was guarded, buried, hidden from the world. Hidden from her. She wondered if anyone had ever seen that side of him. Perhaps no one ever would.

That made her sit up, eyes wide and troubled.

If he wanted her only because he felt guilty, responsible for what had happened to her, she'd have to try to resist him—after all, he might feel guilty now, but once she was whole again, his guilt would surely vanish, and his desire with it. There was something else to consider, too: right now, he needed her to keep Ward Jessup at bay. But if things ever straightened out, he'd have no need of her...and perhaps no desire for her. It would be wise not to get too close to him emotionally. She knew from hard experience that he didn't have a lot of sentiment, even though the loss of his brother had obviously affected him.

Hearing about the baby had affected him, too; Erin didn't doubt that. He was the kind of man who would want children. But when and with whom were questions she couldn't answer. She believed that he'd never completely forgotten what she was like before the wreck. He'd never liked her when she was a model; her beauty had repelled him, antagonized him. But now that she was scarred and crippled, she seemed to appeal to him much more. Why? she wondered. *Why?*

A car door slammed, breaking into the silence, and she tensed, listening. She was wearing a low-cut nightgown with a slit down the side of her scarred hip, and she couldn't bear to have Ty see the way she looked there. But surely he wouldn't come in...would he?

Just as the thought occurred to her, she heard the sound of heavy footsteps coming down the hall. The next instant, the door swung open.

Ty stripped off his gloves as he walked into the room, leaving the door open. "My, my," he murmured, studying the picture she made. "And I thought men only saw mirages in the desert."

"It's more a nightmare than a mirage under the gown," she muttered, scrambling for the covers. "The scar bothers me sometimes, and it stings when fabric rubs against it. The stitches haven't been out long. My hip doesn't like exercise," she couldn't help adding.

"Does it like being dressed in see-through gowns?" he asked, cocking an eyebrow to where she'd pulled up the covers. "That could get it into big trouble. I'd have a talk with it if I were you. While you're about it, you might tell it we're going to exercise it every day, so it might as well stop grumbling."

That didn't sound like the Ty she'd known months

before. His humor was droll these days—not mocking and sarcastic—and he actually seemed to be making an effort to thaw her out. She stared up at him curiously. "Did you get the dog?" she asked.

"No. The damned thing got to the woods and hid, but Jessup's going to pay for that calf all the same." He moved closer to the bed, gripping his gloves in one hand as he walked toward her. He was still wearing the shepherd's coat, although he'd unbuttoned it, and his hat was tilted at an arrogant angle over his face. He stared down at her with narrowed, mocking eyes.

"Something on your mind?" she challenged.

"Yes, and you know what, don't you?" He slapped the gloves against his palm, letting his eyes run over the covers she was huddled under. "Why did you do that?"

She blinked. "Do what?"

"Rush under the blankets like that, the minute I walked in? You haven't got anything I haven't already seen."

She averted her eyes to the blue coverlet. "Maybe not. But you haven't seen it in its present condition, and you're not going to."

"Like hell I'm not."

Even as he said it, he was stripping away the covers. He pinned her to the bed simply by clamping one firm, hard hand down on her waist, and when he sat down beside her, he cut off her last chance at escape.

"No!" she cried as he stripped the gown up to her waist with his free hand, exposing the scarred hip.

It wasn't a pretty sight, despite the fact that it had healed since the wreck. The subsequent surgeries had left more scars, and only a skin graft would restore its former soft smoothness. But the scars didn't bother him—only her attitude toward them.

She closed her eyes because she couldn't bear to see his disgust. "Now are you satisfied?" she asked huskily.

"Not by a long shot, honey." He bent and put his mouth against the scar tissue, felt her stiffen and tremble, heard the involuntary sound that escaped her lips.

"Ty, you mustn't!" she protested, pushing at his head.

He looked up into her wide, frightened green eyes and smiled—actually smiled, although it was mocking and faint and didn't soften the hard face one bit.

"Frightened?" he chided. "Of what? You were terrified that I'd see you like this, so now you know. I'm not disgusted, or horrified, or repulsed. Any more questions?"

She backed up on the pillows and stared at him, heart pounding. "It's gruesome," she said under her breath. "I can't bear to look at it."

"But then you're a cream puff, honey," he said. "I've lived on a ranch all my life. I've seen things and done things that would turn your pretty hair white. By comparison, a few little hairline scars aren't much.''

''They are to me!''

''Considering how you came by them, I guess so,'' he replied, his tone quiet, almost sympathetic. He touched the newest scar gently, where it was still tender. Erin saw his face grow pale, watched his jaw tense as if he were remembering things he didn't want to face.

''Were you in the hospital a long time?'' he asked after a moment.

''After the wreck, yes,'' she confessed, and he flinched. ''Ty—''

''It must have been damned painful,'' he said under his breath, still staring at the scars. ''And with no one to look after you, care about you. God!''

He jerked up from the bed and turned away, his hands rammed into his pockets, the gloves forgotten on the coverlet. His back was ramrod stiff, and there was something disturbing in his stance.

She was just beginning to understand him. It wasn't that he didn't feel anything. He'd just grown adept at hiding his feelings. She remembered what he'd told her about having two strikes against him with women, and she imagined he'd been taunted all his life about his lack of looks. She grimaced at the pain she felt emanating from him.

It was just too much. Her own pain forgotten, she

got out of bed and went to him. Talking wouldn't help, she knew that instinctively. So she went in front of him and slid her arms around his hard waist and pressed against him inside his coat.

He shuddered wildly for an instant. His hands caught her shoulders roughly and hesitated, as if he were thinking about pushing her away. And then the feel of her got through to him, the soft warmth pressed so close to his heart, the scent of her rising into his nostrils.

His hands flattened on her shoulder blades, savoring the feel of her. And he let her come close, let her hold him. His head bent over hers, his cheek finally resting against her hair with a long, aching sigh.

"You're very human after all, aren't you?" she asked softly, her eyes closed as she held him. "You lock it all up inside you and keep people from seeing, but things hurt you just as much as they hurt me. I know you feel bad about what happened, Ty. I'm not bitter anymore. I've stopped hating you for it. Does that help?"

He touched her hair lightly, and his grip didn't slacken one bit. "You see too deeply," he whispered roughly.

"It's like looking in a mirror," she said. "I've done the same thing all my life, too. Locked away the hurts, so no one could see. My father died and my mother started playing the field. One man after another was in and out of her life, and the other kids tormented me with it. You see, their own fathers weren't immune to her. She had affairs with at least two of them.''

His hands tightened around her. ''I guess it was pretty tough.''

''Pure hell.'' She smiled ruefully. ''I grew up near Dallas, remember; I was a small-town Texas girl before I started modeling. Small-town people are the salt of the earth, but they have old-fashioned ideas about morality, and they tend to condemn people who ignore the rules.'' She nuzzled her cheek against the soft cotton of his shirt, feeling the hard muscle and heartbeat underneath. ''I guess that's one reason I never ran around.''

He tugged gently on a strand of her hair. ''At least not until I came along. I guess your conscience gave you hell about that.''

''It did.''

''Oddly enough,'' he said, ''I had some problems with my own conscience. The women I'd...known before weren't virgins.''

''Incredible, isn't it,'' she murmured, ''that I'd get pregnant the very first time?''

''That's what they say happens to good girls.'' He stroked her hair. ''God, I'm sorry, honey,'' he said softly. ''Sorry I wouldn't listen, sorry I didn't go after you. I started to. And before I could, Bruce moved out and fed me a bunch of lies....''

She lifted her head and looked up at him. ''I never

told him about us,'' she said honestly, holding his eyes. ''And I certainly never accused you of...of fumbling.''

''I should have known that, shouldn't I?'' he asked, his voice deep. ''After today, anyway.''

She frowned slightly. ''Why after today?''

He traced her mouth with his finger. ''If you were the kind of woman who'd laugh at a man, you'd have done it today. But you didn't. Instead of making fun of me, you took my hand and showed me how to touch you.''

She blushed and buried her face in his warm throat.

He laughed softly, enjoying that very feminine reaction to his blatant teasing. He tugged lightly on her hair, savoring its softness. ''Men aren't born knowing how to arouse women,'' he said, gently mocking. ''We have to learn. It was exciting, having you show me what you liked. That's never happened for me before.''

''Never?'' she asked without lifting her head.

''Never. Bruce fed you some bull, too, honey, or haven't you cottoned on to that by now?''

''About your sordid reputation and the harem you kept?'' she asked, keeping her red cheeks hidden.

''That's about the size of it,'' he agreed. ''I'm not a virgin, but I've never been much of a rounder. Men who look like I do don't score that often.''

That brought her head up, wide green eyes searching his curiously. "What do you mean, men who look like you do? What's wrong with you?"

He cocked his head a little to one side, staring at her. "I'm ugly."

She smiled, completely without malice. "You're sexy, too," she murmured.

His eyebrows shot up. "Me?"

She dropped her eyes to his chest. "And arrogant," she continued. "Bad-tempered. Impatient..."

"You could have stopped at 'sexy,'" he said.

She shifted restlessly. "No, I couldn't," she said. "We don't want you to get conceited."

"Hip hurting?" he asked softly.

"Nagging a bit." She peeked up at him. "I'll be your best friend if you'll stop making me do those exercises."

"No deal. You're going to walk again even if I become your worst enemy. Here." He swung her up into his arms without warning and carried her back to bed.

She clung, drowning in the masculine scent of him, the feel of that powerful, lean body. "You're very strong," she murmured absently.

"I don't sit behind a desk and count my money. I work for what I've got." He put her down on the coverlet, and as he rose up, his eyes caressed the curves of her body like seeking hands.

She didn't try to cover herself, although part of one creamy breast was revealed by her disheveled gown.

She let him look, glorying unashamed in the pleasure she saw in his silver-gray eyes.

"Have you ever let another man look at you like this?" he asked, his voice deep and faintly cutting.

"No," she said.

"Bruce wanted to, didn't he?" he asked, lifting his eyes to hers. "He wanted that and a hell of a lot more."

"He never got it," she replied, her eyes steady, intent. "I never felt that way about him. He was my friend, until he started wanting more than I could give him. I had no idea he was that obsessed with marrying me until the day after I left here the first time. He…he raved like a lunatic about the way you looked at me," she confided hesitantly. "I tried to tell him that you didn't even like me, but he wouldn't listen." She lowered her eyes. "I'm sorry, if that helps. I wouldn't have caused trouble between you for anything."

"Bruce and I had never been close. We were raised separately and he was six years younger. He always tried to compete with me. He had to have the fastest car, the most expensive clothes, the finest house." He shrugged. "I never cared about those things. I have money, but I'd do as well without it. I'd rather have a good horse and a day's work ahead of me than sit in some damned restaurant putting on airs for other people."

She searched his hard face. "I think I liked that

about you most of all, even at first," she said. "You were never a snob. Bruce was."

"I know," he replied slowly.

"Why did he want to cause trouble?" she asked. "He knew you disliked me. Why tell a lot of lies?"

"Because he sensed that there was something under the dislike." He stared down at her. "He knew that I wanted you."

Her heart jumped. "I didn't. Not until that night." She lowered embarrassed eyes to the coverlet. "I'm sorry I disappointed you," she added hesitantly. "I didn't know much."

"You didn't disappoint me," he snapped angrily. "That was all bad temper and Bruce's lies!"

His vehemence startled her. She looked up into blazing silver eyes. "I didn't?" she asked.

"I think you were a hell of a lot more disappointed than I was." He watched her intently. "You got nothing out of it except pain and a baby that I cost you with my black temper."

She shook her head. "The baby wasn't meant to be," she said gently. And she meant it...now. Seeing his guilt had knocked the bitterness out of her once and for all. "You can't spend your whole life blaming yourself for it."

"Can't I?" he asked coldly.

"You'll get married someday," she said, hating the thought even as it was forming. "You'll have other children."

He took a cigarette from his pocket and lit it. "Will I? Sure, maybe I could advertise: 'Rich man with no looks seeking wife....'"

"Don't," she said, grimacing.

"I told you, I'm realistic. No woman is ever going to want me—unless it's for my money. So why not lay it on the line at the outset?" he asked with a mocking smile.

"All right, if you're going to wallow in self-pity, maybe I will, too," she shot back, infuriated with him. "I'm scarred and crippled, and no longer a virgin. So maybe now that I'm independently wealthy, I could use the same kind of ad for myself!"

His face went hard. The cigarette poised in midair, inches away from his lips. "Those scars won't matter to any man who cares about you."

"And how about my scarlet past and my stiff leg?" she continued, sitting up straight. The bodice of her gown was slipping, but she was too angry to notice.

Ty wasn't. "How about your exquisite breasts?" he murmured, watching one that was all but exposed to his hungry gaze.

"Ty!" she gasped, sidetracked by the expression in his face.

"They are exquisite, too," he said softly. "You can't imagine what a hell of a time I'm having trying to stand here and smoke my cigarette. So would you mind pulling that up—" he nodded toward her bodice

"—before I come down there and make a grab for you?"

She tugged the strap up again, coloring prettily for what seemed like the tenth time. "Do you really want to make a grab for me, the way I look?"

"Especially the way you look," he replied, lifting the cigarette to his faintly smiling mouth. "I still ache from having to leave you here in the first place. It's a damned good thing Grandy chose that particular time to tell me about the dog."

She glanced toward him and away. "Is it?"

"I'd say so," he replied, staring at her intently. "Considering that you're not on the Pill and I didn't have anything to use."

"I thought men were always prepared."

"Was I prepared the last time?" He laughed roughly. "My God, Erin, do you realize how small Ravine is? There's a lady clerk at the drugstore—Mrs. Blake, whom I've known since I was ten years old—and I can just imagine her expression if I walked up to her to buy something like that, when she knows I'm a bachelor and you're in the house with me."

Her lips parted. "Oh."

"Oh, indeed. No wonder there are so many unplanned pregnancies. Kids these days don't practice restraint, and most boys that age are too damned shy to walk into a drugstore and buy what they need. So they trust it all to luck." He took a long draw from his cigarette. "You and I aren't kids, but we know the consequences all too well now, don't we?"

"I didn't plan to...to do that with you," she faltered, averting her gaze.

"Neither did I. But we were both half-starved for each other, and completely alone, and we knew it. I should have protected you. I did try," he said softly. "But it was too much. It had been such a long time for me, and I'd wanted you until it was just short of obsession."

That was shocking. And interesting. "A long time?" she asked, looking up.

He smiled at her ruefully. "About two years, if you're curious; I told you I had hangups."

She liked that. She even smiled a little shyly. "Well, I never had."

"I noticed," he murmured.

She glanced up again, then down at her folded hands. "Have you...since?"

"I told you in the car. No. And I haven't wanted to." He finished the cigarette and crushed it out in the ashtray on the bedside table. "I don't want anyone else. I'd rather have the memory of you, that night, than the reality of any other woman in the world."

She couldn't help it. Her eyes brimmed with tears that trickled onto her silky cheeks while she stared at him spellbound.

"Little watering pot," he chided. He pulled out a handkerchief and dabbed it clumsily at her eyes.

"Stop that. The only way I could possibly comfort you wouldn't be sensible, with you in that damned little see-through gown."

"Coward." She smiled at him through her tears.

"You bet, honey; in that respect, at least." He gave her the handkerchief and paused to pick up his gloves. He stared at her with narrowed eyes while she blew her nose and wiped away the last of the tears. "Erin, what you said at the doctor's office—does the talk about you and me really bother you?"

She looked up, surprised. "Are people really talking?"

He sighed. "I'm afraid so. One of the men mentioned something he'd heard." He didn't tell her that the man had mentioned it himself, because he'd had one drink too many, or that Ty had planted a hard fist right in the middle of his face and fired him seconds later.

She shifted quietly on the bed. "Well, there's nothing to be done about it," she said after a minute. "I own half the property, as things stand. I can't leave without hurting a lot of people."

"There's one thing we could do," he said, staring at his dusty boots.

"What?"

He turned his boot and looked at the mud on the sole. "We've already agreed that I may grow old trying to find a woman who'll have me, what with my looks. And you don't seem too confident about getting a man. And neither of us has slept with anyone else since the night before you left." He glanced at her. "Maybe we could learn to get along, if we worked at it. And the will doesn't really leave us much choice. You'll be here for life."

She knew what he was going to say. She could refuse. It would be the sensible thing to do. But part of her was still powerfully attracted to him. She liked lying in his hard arms, being touched and kissed and held by him. She responded to his strength, his stubbornness. She'd never want anyone else. And although he didn't love her, he'd at least look after her; she knew that instinctively. Perhaps in time things would work out. There could be children....

She cocked her head and stared at him. "Would you want children?" she asked levelly.

"If you're asking me to give you a child to replace the one you lost, yes. I can do that. Not now," he added, studying her body. "You're not in any condition to carry one. But we can have children, if that's what you want."

It sounded as if he weren't all that enthusiastic about it. Could she have been wrong about him? Did he not want a family? Or did he want one so badly that he was just hiding his feelings, afraid of being hurt?

She fiddled with the coverlet, thinking.

"You're stuck here, thanks to your conscience,"

he reminded her. "You might as well have my name as well as half my ranch."

"Thanks," she said curtly. "What a sweet proposal of marriage!"

"Well, take it or leave it, then!" he replied hotly. "I'm not all that thrilled myself, but it's the only solution I see."

"I won't sleep with you!"

"Sleep in the damned barn, for all I care." His face was harder than rock, his eyes blazing.

Erin's lower lip trembled, and she tugged the covers up higher. How in the world had it come to this so suddenly?

"If you marry me, you'll do it in a church," she said doggedly. "I'm not getting married by any justice of the peace."

His eyebrows arched. "Did I ask you to?"

"And I don't want a social event, either. Just a small wedding." She looked at her slender, ringless hands. "And I don't want my mother there. She'd make a circus out of it."

He relaxed a little. "Okay."

"And I don't want to have to walk down the aisle dragging my leg behind me."

"After we've done those exercises for a few weeks, you won't be dragging it behind you," he told her. "You'll improve. But it's going to take time and effort and hard work. And no backsliding."

"Tyrant," she muttered. "All right, I'll do it, even if I curl up and die of pain."

"When?" he asked, his voice strangely husky, his eyes searching hers.

"When do you want to?" she asked warily.

"Next week." When she gasped, he added, "Well, that's how it has to be unless you want newspaper coverage. I'm newsworthy—homely face and all."

"You are not homely; will you please stop running yourself down?" she asked, exasperated.

"If you'll stop talking about your gimpy leg, I'll stop talking about my homely mug," he replied.

"Done."

"Want a diamond?" he asked.

"No. Just a plain gold band."

"Have it your own way." He turned and started out the door.

"That's it?" she queried, astonished. "That's all?"

"What else do you want?" he asked reasonably. "If I get down on my knees on that cold floor, there's a good chance I'll be stuck there until spring. And kissing you to seal the engagement wouldn't make much sense, either, with you lying there naked."

"I am not naked!"

"As good as," he replied. "So I'm doing the decent thing and getting out of here, like a thoughtful prospective bridegroom. Don't stay up too late. We want to get a good start on those exercises in the morning. Sleep tight, now.'' And he closed the door behind him.

She stared at the door for a moment, openmouthed. What a proposal! What an ardent bridegroom! She only wished she had some priceless Ming vase or something to fling at the door. She lay back, and with a muffled curse, pulled the covers over her head.

Ty, meanwhile, was walking down the long hallway whistling softly, his face animated, full of life— and almost handsome. He grinned and then he laughed. It was going to be a long, hard road, but he'd taken the first step. He was going to make up to her for every horrible thing that had happened. He was going to spoil her rotten. He opened the door to his own room and went in. Sleep would be a long time coming, he knew.

But he didn't even care.

Seven

Erin had hoped that being engaged would change Ty. Not so. He was the same as before, right down to the purely domineering way he made her do the hated exercises and stood over her the whole while.

"Why don't you do them too?" she grumbled a few mornings later as he was drilling her.

"My hip isn't busted," he explained patiently. "A little higher, honey; you aren't stretching far enough."

He never used to use endearments, but now he was calling her "honey" every chance he got. She smiled a little at that telling change of character. Well, she conceded, perhaps he had changed a bit. He was more relaxed since she'd been at the ranch, more approachable. She studied him while she did the bicycle exercise and thought that he didn't even seem all that homely to her anymore. He was a striking man physically, and he had beautiful hands—long-fingered, lean and elegant, darkly tanned like the rest of him, with flat nails and a sprinkling of dark hair on the backs.

"Take a picture," he advised, catching her appraisal. "It'll scare off the crows."

"Shame on you," she chided. "I was just admiring your manly physique, not criticizing you."

"You're not bad yourself," he murmured, smiling faintly as he ran his eyes over her body. "That burgundy thing you're wearing looks good on you."

"Thank you," she said, surprised by the compliment. "It's called a leotard."

"What are you going to get married in?" he asked between sips of coffee.

"Well," she began, panting as she sat up and wiped her face with a towel, "I have a beige streetlength dress—"

"The hell you say," he interrupted hotly.

She stared at him, uncomprehending. "What's the matter with you?"

"White, that's what," he returned shortly. He put the cup down and kneeled beside her. "White. No beige or green or gray. You get married in a white dress."

Her face colored. "I don't have the right anymore," she murmured.

"It was me," he said levelly, although his eyes were flashing. "I remember exactly what you looked like, and how new it was to you. The instant it happened, I was looking straight into your eyes. I even remember how it felt: white."

She swallowed. "White," she said slowly, shaken by the passion in his voice, his eyes.

"No man ever had a sweeter virgin," he breathed, looking at her mouth. "No man ever enjoyed an initiation as much as I enjoyed that one. There's never been anyone but me, and we both know it. In the eyes of God, that married us as surely as any minister will, and nobody's going to shame you out of your white wedding dress. Not even your own little puritan conscience."

She managed a smile. "You're a nice man sometimes."

"I haven't had much practice at being nice," he confessed, toying with the sleeve of her leotard. "I grew up pretty alone, and I've been that way most of my life. I never mixed well. I still don't."

He was so different in these rare moods. So approachable. She reached out hesitantly and touched the back of his hand, letting her fingers learn the hair-roughened skin, the long, elegant fingers.

"Nicotine stains," she murmured, seeing the yellow between his forefinger and his middle finger. "Why do you smoke so much?"

"I only do it when I'm strung out, living on my nerves," he said quietly, looking straight into her eyes. "You do that to me. Having you around, being near you."

She smiled. "I can't imagine anything or anyone making you nervous, least of all me."

"Think so? Look." He held out his hand, and she saw that it was trembling slightly.

Shocked, she looked up into his eyes and saw the flames there, burning steadily, consuming. Suddenly she understood. "Oh, Ty..." she breathed.

"That's why you shouldn't carouse around here in see-through gowns," he murmured, smiling at his own vulnerability. "I'm a case when I get close to you."

She searched his silvery eyes quietly. So it hadn't been easy for him, either. His conscience had hurt because of the way things had happened. The loss of the baby disturbed him, Bruce's death had hurt, was still hurting probably. He'd had his own share of grief and guilt, yet he'd come himself to bring her back to Staghorn, forced her to feel again, bullied her into caring about her health. And she'd given him nothing except a hard time. Bruce had done this to them, out of misplaced love and blazing jealousy...but it was time to let go of the past and take responsibility for the future. Their future. It was too late to dwell on what might have been if Bruce hadn't interfered.

"After we're married," she said softly, choosing her words with exquisite care and looking into his eyes the whole time, "I'll let you have me."

A visible shudder went through his strong body. "You don't realize what you're saying," he said.

"So far, you've done most of the giving," she replied. "You've lost Bruce and part of your inheritance and been stuck with me to boot. You've made me go on living when I wanted to die. I think it's time I gave you something."

His jaw tensed. He got to his feet and moved away. "That's something we can discuss another time."

"I've set you off again." She sighed. "Oh, Ty, won't you ever learn not to blow up every time I say something personal?"

"Sure," he returned, wheeling, "when you stop offering me charity. I don't want your body in return for a roof over your head."

"I didn't mean it like that!"

"I don't want you that way," he said shortly. "Not as some damned sacrifice."

She shook her head. "You are the most maddening man," she said. "Just when I think I'm beginning to understand you... Okay, have it your own way. I'll sleep in the barn with the rats."

"I don't have rats in the barn," he said absently.

"Why not?"

"My king snake lives in there. He eats them."

She swallowed. "I take back my offer to sleep in the barn."

"It's just an old king snake. He wouldn't hurt you."

"Fear of snakes runs in my family," she told him. "I think my great-grandfather was eaten by one. He was a war correspondent. He disappeared in the jungles of South America, and his skeleton was found years later, they said, lying inside the skeleton of a monstrous python."

"A grisly end, all right," he agreed. "But king snakes don't eat people."

"That's what you say." She grimaced as she moved. "Damn these exercises! They get worse every day."

"You'll work the kinks out in a week or so. It will get easier, believe me."

"Why do have to keep this up?" she groaned. "I'll never be able to model again, especially if I'm married."

He stared at her. "Won't you? Why not?"

"You'd let me work?" she asked, surprised.

"You're a human being, not my unpaid slave," he replied. "I don't believe in shackling a woman to the stove and keeping her pregnanant. You're free to do whatever you want, except sleep with other men."

"I wouldn't want to do that," she said.

He laughed shortly. "No, I guess not. It must have

been a pretty big disappointment.'' He turned back toward the door, lighting another cigarette as he went.

She gaped at him until she realized what he'd meant. Without giving herself time to think, she reached behind the easy chair, picked up one of his boots, and hurled it after him. It hit the wall instead of him, but it got his attention.

He stared at it as if he'd just found a dead fish on the carpet. He picked it up, looked at it, and turned to face Erin.

''Did you throw a boot at me?''

''Of course I did.''

''Did you mean to hit the wall?''

''No,'' she said calmly. ''I was aiming for your head.''

''You could use a little practice,'' he observed.

''Not really. As big as your feet are, I could aim at a wall and still hit you if I tried hard enough.''

He glared at her. ''I do not have big feet.''

''Neither do ducks.''

He came back toward her, holding the boot, and the look in his eyes wasn't all that friendly.

She scrambled to her feet, grimacing and hobbling as she tried to get behind a barrier, any barrier. ''No, go away!'' she cried. ''I'm crippled!''

''Not yet,'' he muttered, ''but it's a distinct possibility.''

''Ty! You wouldn't hit me!''

''Wouldn't I?'' He grabbed her roughly around the

waist, lifting her. "Now how brave do you feel?" he asked.

She shifted in his tight hold. "Put me down and I'll tell you."

"Stop squirming or you'll get put down the hard way." He looked into her eyes from an unnerving proximity. "Were your eyes always that shade of green?"

"I guess so."

"They look like leaves in early spring," he murmured, "just after the dew glazes them."

"Yours are like silver when you get mad," she told him. "And your eyelashes are almost as long as mine."

His eyes left hers, traveling slowly down to her mouth and lingering there. "Even thin as a rail and half dead, you're beautiful."

"I'm not, but thank you for saying so." She felt his breath, and her body reacted violently to his nearness. "I like the way your mouth feels when you kiss me," she said, half under her breath. "It's very hard and a little rough, and..." She moaned under the warm crush of his lips, stiffening, arching up against his hard chest, her arms clasping his neck violently.

If he was rough, so was she. She loved the feel of his muscular body, the male scent of him. Her mouth opened to taste more of his, and she moaned again as he took full advantage of that vulnerability.

He began to tremble, and she felt a twinge of guilt

for inciting him. He didn't want her this way, and she shouldn't have thrown him off balance. But it was exciting to know she had such power over him.

She forced her throbbing body to be still, and her mouth gentled under his. Her fingers stroked his cheek, his hair, soothing him, as her lips moved to his cheeks, his nose, his closed eyes, his eyebrows. He was still trembling, but he didn't move, he didn't protest. He let her do what she wanted; stood quietly and let her explore his rough features.

"I'm sorry," she whispered as her lips moved back to his and brushed them apologetically. "I can't help it. When you touch me, I go crazy."

"I guess that makes two of us," he said gruffly. His eyes opened and looked into hers. "You're pretty wild when we make love. I never dreamed you'd be so uninhibited with me."

"Neither did I," she told him. Her mouth touched his cheek, opening, caressing. "I want...to do so...many shocking things with you."

He bit her lower lip gently, feeling her go taut at the tiny caress. "I ache," he whispered.

"So do I." She moved her breasts against his chest and whimpered a little with suppressed passion.

"Erin, if we don't stop now, we may not be able to. I wasn't this worked up the night I took you."

She let her forehead rest on his broad shoulder. "Neither was I," she said unsteadily. "But we've only been kissing."

"Not quite." He nuzzled his cheek against hers. "Move your breasts against me like that again."

She did, feeling them swell and go hard, feeling his sudden rigidity. "I don't want to hurt you," she whispered.

"You can't imagine what a sweet hurt it is." He drew her against him as he let her slide to her feet and feel every inch of him on the way down. His legs trembled a little at her nearness. "A kind of throbbing ache…"

"I want you," she said huskily, closing her eyes as his hands slid down to her hips and urged her even nearer.

"I want you, too," he replied. "But we can't. Not like this. It's too big a risk."

She sighed. "I guess so."

"It isn't my body saying that," he added dryly. "Only my mind."

She laughed at that, and the tension between them eased a little. "Is that so?"

He drew in a steadying breath and moved her away enough to satisfy her modesty. "We're getting married Tuesday," he reminded her. "I guess we can survive until then."

"I guess." She studied a loose button on his shirt and thought that after they were married, she could take better care of him. Sew on buttons and iron his shirts and wash his clothes—such intimate little things that were suddenly of earthshaking importance. She could even sleep in his arms....

She flushed, and he saw it and smiled.

"What brought that on?" he teased.

"Nothing."

He kissed her forehead tenderly. "You can sleep in my bed if you want to, after we're married," he whispered.

She felt hot all over. "Can I?" she asked. Her voice sounded breathless, wildly excited. She felt that way, too.

"All the time," he said huskily. "I can watch you undress, and you can watch me. We can touch each other. We can make love."

She trembled helplessly. "In the light?" she asked, looking up.

"In the light," he whispered, his voice urgent, deep. "Did you talk to the doctor about the Pill?"

"Yes. I..." She cleared her throat. It was hard to talk about something so intimate. She looked at his shirt instead. "It has to be started at a particular time, which...which I did two days ago," she faltered.

He chuckled softly. "I'm a cattleman," he whispered at her ear. "I know all about cycles and ovulation and 'that time of the month.'"

"Oh." She went really scarlet then and couldn't have looked at him to save her soul.

"Erin, it's part of life." He tilted her chin up, forcing her eyes to meet his. "There's nothing in marriage that should be taboo for a man and woman to discuss. I want honesty more than anything. I'll never lie to you, and I'll expect the same courtesy. I don't want you to be afraid to talk to me about anything that disturbs you.''

"I never had anyone to talk to about sex," she whispered as if it were some deep, dark secret. ''My mother did it all the time, but she was too embarrassed to discuss it with me. Everything I learned was from gossiping with other girls and reading books.''

He smoothed her hair. ''And with me,'' he added quietly.

''And with you,'' she agreed. ''It was so intimate....'' She hesitated.

''Talk to me,'' he urged. ''Don't bottle it up.''

He made it so easy, so natural. She toyed with the loose button on his shirt. It was a nice shirt, a brown check, and it moved when he breathed. She could see the swell of his muscles and the dark shadow of hair underneath it. ''I'm sorry I fought you at the last,'' she whispered.

''You didn't expect it to hurt that much.''

She raised her eyes. ''No. Nobody told me. I thought it would just be uncomfortable.''

''It probably would have been, if I hadn't been so hungry for you,'' he told her. ''Women take a lot of arousing. But my education in that department is sadly lacking. Knowing the mechanics is one thing; putting them into practice is another. Put simply,'' he murmured, searching her eyes, "I know how to have sex. But I don't know how to make love. There's one hell of a difference."

"You never felt…you never wanted to do that with other women?" she asked.

He smiled, shaking his head.

She smiled back shyly. "I'm glad."

He brushed her hair away from her collar. "Didn't you ever want a man to make love to you?"

"Yes," she said, touching his shirt pocket gently. "I wanted you to, from the first time I saw you. It frightened me a little, because you didn't even like me."

"Like hell I didn't," he said gently. "I wanted you desperately."

"But you were horrible to me!"

"Sure I was," he said. "I didn't think you'd look twice at a face like mine."

So that was it. It had all been defensive on his part, and, as his father had taught him, the best defense was a good offense. She searched his hard face. "Bruce said you hated me."

His eyes darkened. "I know. I read the letters. It wasn't true. He played on my ego for all he was worth." He took one of her hands in his and stared at it for a long moment. "He said you laughed at me. At the way I was with you."

She shook her head slowly, deliberately. "That was the biggest lie of all."

He touched her face with gentle, searching fingers. "I'm sorry that I hurt you," he said. "That was the last thing I wanted, despite what I said at the time."

She felt like a young girl again, all shyness and excitement. "It wasn't all that bad," she told him. "I liked...touching you."

He remembered her hands, slowly exploring, feeling the hard contours of his body, deliciously uninhibited. He began to tremble. "God!"

"Ty..." She looked up with tormented eyes.

"Come here," he said roughly, pulling her hard against him, wrapping her up in a bearish embrace. "Come close. They say it helps if you hold each other until the ache goes away."

She closed her eyes and felt the rigidity slowly draining out of both of them. She was reminded of a particular passage in a book about lovemaking she'd once read. If a woman wasn't satisfied, it had said, she could ease the ache by being held very hard. Somehow Ty had known this.

"Do you read books about sex?" she asked.

"Sure," he replied dryly. "Don't you?"

"Not a lot," she confessed. "I found out more by listening to some of my girlfriends."

"What wild lives they must lead."

"You wouldn't believe it!" And she told him some of their adventures, right down to the scandalous details.

"For a shy girl, you tell a good story," he said, laughing. "Feeling better now?"

"Uh-huh," she murmured. "Are you?"

"I guess I'll live." He let her go reluctantly, looking into the softness of her eyes, enjoying the vivid alertness of her face. "What a change," he remarked, "from the pale little ghost I found in that New York apartment."

"I was pretty down," she admitted. "Life wasn't offering much just then."

He took both her hands in his. "I'll make it up to you," he said. "All of it, every bit."

"Ty…"

"Soak in a hot tub for a while, now," he advised, letting her go. "I have some outside work to get through. Later, I'll ride into Ravine with you and we'll pick out a wedding ring."

"All right." She watched him leave, her eyes soft and caring. Things were changing so rapidly. And what had begun as a trial, a fearful readjustment, was fast becoming the greatest joy of her life. She felt all the pain and bitterness draining out of her, being replaced by a growing excitement and feeling of closeness.

If only she could believe that he really felt something for her, something more than pity and desire and a need to make restitution for what he'd done to her. It was so difficult to read him, even now. She didn't want pity or guilt from him. She thought about the tenderness of his hands, the hungry roughness of his mouth... She wanted him, that was undeniable. But she wanted something else as well. She wanted him to...need her. Yes. Need her. Because she... needed him. There was another word, too, a deeper word. But she was afraid to even think it. That would come later, perhaps, if things worked out.

She went back to the hated exercises for the first time without being told. She had to get back on her feet, she had to be whole again; because it was imperative that she show him she could stand alone. Then, if he still turned to her after that, without pity and without guilt...then there might be the hope of something deeper between them.

But until he saw her as a woman, and not some crippled songbird with a broken spirit, she could never be sure of him—or herself.

Eight

Ty and Erin were married in a quiet ceremony in the small Presbyterian church where the Wades had worshiped for two generations.

Erin wore a white street-length dress with long sleeves and a high neckline. She'd hoped that she wouldn't need her cane, but it was still difficult to walk without it.

Ty was wearing a well-tailored three-piece suit, and he looked debonair and worldly. He towered over Erin, even though she wore high heels, and she felt small and vulnerable standing next to him.

A handful of people witnessed the ceremony, including Ty's foreman, Stuart Grandy, Conchita and

José, and a few neighbors. It only took a few minutes, and as Ty slid the small circle of gold onto her finger, he brushed his lips gently against her mouth in a kiss that was more promise than reality.

Erin felt tears burning her eyes, and she tried desperately not to cry. Ty seemed to realize that her emotions were in turmoil because he smiled at her and produced a handkerchief as well-wishers gathered around them.

"Well, somebody had to cry at my wedding," she said, dabbing her eyes, "and who better than me?"

"I'd cry, too, if I had to marry him," declared Red Davis, one of Ty's cowhands.

Ty glared at him. "There went your Christmas bonus."

Red grinned. He was only in his early twenties, and full of rowdy humor. "Think so? In that case, wait until tonight, boss."

"You set one foot on my homestead and I'll load my Winchester," Ty told him.

"Reverend Bill, did you hear what he just said?" Red called out to the tall, bespectacled minister. "He says he's going to shoot me!"

"I never!" Ty said, looking shocked.

Reverend Bill Gates chuckled as he joined them. "I heard why he said that, Red, and if you go onto his porch, I'll lend him some buckshot for his shotgun."

Red shook his head sorrowfully. "Shame on you."

Bill grinned. "Shame on you."

Ty took Erin's hand in his and braced himself for all the congratulations. She wondered if he found this as much of an ordeal as she did. She wasn't all that comfortable in public yet, with her scars still visible and her self-confidence shot to pieces. But she leaned on Ty instead of the cane and forced herself to smile.

Eventually, they returned to Staghorn for the reception. Conchita had taken care of all the details, and had even hired a caterer to help so that there would be plenty of food. It seemed to take forever for the guests to eat their fill, and by then Ty was into a heavy discussion with two of the neighboring ranchers about the growing number of oil fields in the area.

Erin felt guilty for being so irritable, but she was fuming long before the last piece of cake had been finished off. She went into the kitchen with Conchita and helped her wash dishes.

"Is not right," Conchita grumbled, glaring down at *la señora*. "On your wedding day, this is not the proper thing for you to be doing."

"That's right," Erin agreed. "So you wade in there and tell my new husband that."

"Not me," Conchita replied. "I like my job."

"You and I could take this terrific dishwashing routine on the stage," she told the housekeeper. "We'd make a fortune."

Conchita stared at her, round-eyed. "Perhaps it is the fever."

"I don't have a fever."

"No?" Conchita grinned, her teeth a flash of white in her dark face.

Erin flushed and grabbed at a dishtowel. "I'll dry."

"As you wish, señora."

Ty found them there half an hour later. He stopped in the doorway, watching. "What a hell of a way to spend your wedding day," he said shortly.

"No, it's not," Erin replied, smiling poisonously over her shoulder. "It's super. Conchita and I are going to take this great act on the stage. We'll win awards."

"I wouldn't buy a ticket."

"You're just jealous because nobody would pay to watch you and Mr. Hawes and Mr. Danson stand around and talk oil and cattle for two hours."

"So that's it," he murmured.

"Now you will get an insight into the true nature of woman," Conchita informed him, putting her dishtowel aside. "Go off and fight, and then you can make up properly. José is taking me in to town to shop for Christmas, so you will have the house all to yourselves."

They waited, glaring at each other in silence, until she'd left the kitchen.

"I don't want to make up with you," she told him furiously.

"So stay in here and pout," he replied. "I can always go work off my temper with the men."

"Good! Why don't you start a fight? Maybe I could sell tickets to that!"

He glared at her one last time, turned on his heel, grabbed his Stetson, slammed it onto his head, and stomped off toward the porch. The door crashed loudly behind him.

Erin flung a plate at the door. Unfortunately, it was one of those new unbreakable ones, and it only made a loud thud, not a satisfying shatter. She sighed and picked it up to wash it again. By the time she'd finished, tears were streaming down her cheeks.

Ty stayed away all day. Conchita and José came home to find Erin in her own room and Ty outside with his men. They stared at each other for a moment and then shook their heads as they went about their business.

By early evening, Erin had taken a bath and settled into her bed, two short novels by her side. At eight-thirty she unlocked the door to Conchita, who bustled in with a bowl of homemade soup and some hot coffee. Erin closed her ears to Conchita's well-meant grumbling and in the process forgot to relock the door behind the housekeeper. She ate the soup, drank the coffee, and finished the second novel, by which time she had a genuine headache and a throbbing hip. She felt thoroughly miserable. She wished she'd never met Ty in the first place; she was sure that she hated him. Somewhere along the way she drifted off to sleep, tears drying on her cheeks.

Ty came in about midnight, dirty and disheveled and half out of humor, and found her asleep in her own room. He glared at her sleeping form for a long moment before he closed the door again and went to his room to spend a cold, unsatisfying night by himself.

The next morning, Erin was up before breakfast, exercising by herself in the living room. She'd show him! She'd get better, then she'd leave him! She'd go back to work and make a fortune and have men running after her all over the place, and then he'd be sorry! The thought gave her fresh energy. She was going full steam when Ty walked into the room, smoking a cigarette.

"Good morning," he said.

"Good morning," she replied sweetly. "I hope you had a horrible night?"

"I did, thanks. How about you?"

"I hardly slept."

"You were sawing logs when I came home," he remarked.

"Oh, then you did finally come home?" she asked sarcastically. "How kind of you."

"You started it," he muttered.

"No, you did." She glared at him. "Ignoring me like that in front of everybody, letting me go off and wash dishes on my wedding day! How could you!"

He took a deep breath. "I've been a bachelor for thirty-four years, and I'll remind you that this is no conventional love match. We got married to keep gossip down, didn't we? Or is there a reason I don't know about?''

He was right. She stared at him blankly while she went over their relationship in her mind. Then she forced herself to compare that reality to the idyllic little fantasy of mutual love she'd created. Finally she lowered her eyes.

"I'm sorry," she said dully. "I had no right to get upset like that. We did get married to keep gossip down, after all.''

He was sorry he'd opened his mouth when he saw the life drain out of her. All the lovely brightness, all the excitement that had given her such beauty yesterday...gone. He hadn't thought about it from her point of view. Women took things so seriously. His eyes narrowed as he watched her sitting there, slightly stooped, and it suddenly occurred to him that she might have expected him to behave like a...well, like a bridegroom. He'd been so busy trying not to frighten her that he'd obviously gone overboard. Now she thought he didn't want her, that he didn't care.

"Did you want me last night?" he asked gently.

"No," she said.

He knelt beside her and tilted her chin up, forcing her wounded eyes to meet his.

"Yes," she mumbled.

"Then why didn't you say so?" he asked.

"What did you expect me to do, walk up to you

in the middle of a discussion on artificial insemination and tell you I wanted to make love? I'm sure your neighbors would have found that interesting.''

He smiled faintly. ''I guess they would have.'' He touched her hair, feeling its dampness. ''I don't know much about being a husband. You'll have to bear with me until I get the hang of it.''

She searched his eyes. ''Maybe I'm just expecting more from you than you want to give. Things have never been normal for us. I've been so confused....''

''And so hurt.'' He grimaced. ''And I seem to do more of it every day. Hurting you is the last thing I want.''

''And pity is the last thing I want.'' She touched his hand where it rested on her shoulder. ''I'm having some problems with this hip.'' Well, that's almost the truth, she told herself; it does ache. ''It's made me irritable. I'm sorry I've made things difficult for you. I won't be troublesome anymore, I promise.'' She got to her feet, moving away from him, oblivious to the stunned look on his face. ''What Conchita said yesterday reminded me that I haven't done any Christmas shopping, either. I don't relish walking around a lot, but I need to buy some things. Could you spare someone to drive me over to San Antonio?''

His face hardened. ''I'll drive you myself,'' he said coldly. ''When do you want to go?''

''Saturday would be fine.''

''All right.'' He turned and left her without another

word. She didn't let herself think about why. She wasn't going to beg for his attention; if he didn't care enough to give it, she'd learn to live without it. Somehow.

It was a long week, during which she and Ty met at the table and nowhere else. She found things to keep her busy, as did he, and they communicated only when it was absolutely necessary. Conchita just shook her head and mumbled, but she was too wary of Ty to come right out and say anything. His temper went from bad to worse. Erin could hear him out at the corral, giving people hell for everything from leaving gates open to breathing. She felt responsible, and she kept out of his way as much as she could. The marriage that had started out with such promise was turning into a fiasco.

Finally Saturday came, and Ty was ready, as promised, to escort Erin to San Antonio. He looked rich and important in his cream-colored dress Stetson and boots—and every inch the Texan in faded jeans and a denim jacket. Erin felt a little dowdy beside him in a simple gray jersey dress. She didn't have many clothes, but she wasn't going to spend money buying new ones. She still didn't feel entitled to her share of the ranch, despite the will and everything that had happened to her because of the Wades. She'd never forgotten what Ty had said in the car, how he'd accused her of wanting to live off him. She didn't realize that he hadn't actually meant what he'd said, so she'd taken the words at face value.

"Is there any particular place you'd like to go?" Ty asked politely as they reached the outskirts of the city.

"I don't care," she murmured, staring out the window at the sprawling metropolis. Despite the fact that a million or so people lived in San Antonio, it seemed nicely spread out except for right downtown near the Alamo Plaza. At least there were plenty of parking lots around, she thought.

"It's a big city," he said. "It would help if I knew what you wanted to shop for. Are you looking for new clothes?"

"Why? Do I look like I need some?" she asked, glaring at him.

"You wear that same dress every time we go out," he remarked. "It's wearing on my eyes."

"Then by all means, I'll buy another one," she said coldly.

"Go ahead, take it personally," he said, his eyes never leaving the road. "Better yet, why don't you sit down and cry? That would make me feel even worse than I already do."

She bit her lower lip hard as sidewalks and pedestrians blurred past the window of the Lincoln. "I haven't had money to spend on clothes."

He glanced at her angrily. "Do you know what

Staghorn is worth at current market prices?'' he demanded.

''I am not spending your money on clothes. I'll spend what I made modeling.''

''For God's sake! What the—''

He broke off as a parking lot caught his attention, near the Alamo. He pulled into the last vacant spot and parked before he turned to her with blazing silver eyes.

''Now look here...'' he began. Then he caught the glimmer of tears in her eyes, despite the fact that her face was averted. Instantly he calmed down. He reached for one of her hands, tightly clenched on her purse, and pried it loose. It was soft and slender and very cool. He touched her pulse and found it was racing wildly.

Erin jerked her hand away and glared at him.

''Could we go shopping, please?''

''Yes, I think it's about time we did,'' he murmured. ''And I know the perfect spot for it.''

He took her arm and escorted her down the street, into an elegant old hotel. She watched, wide-eyed, as he booked a room, then drew the manager off to one side and murmured something. A minute later, he took the key, signed the register, and led her into the elevator.

The room was old but elegant, done up in shades of green with all the modern furnishings coordinated to please the eye. And there was a huge king-size bed.

"What are we doing here?" she asked hesitantly.

He locked the door and laid the key on the dresser before he turned toward her, his eyes as deep and mysterious as a winter day. "I'll give you three guesses," he said, moving toward her.

Her breath caught in her throat. She couldn't move. He took her purse away from her and then proceeded to undress her.

"You and I need a lot of privacy." He removed the dress and her slip and laid them aside. "We haven't had it at the ranch. But we'll have it here."

She swallowed. "We're going to…to…?"

"Yes." He bent and put his mouth softly over hers, feeling it tremble. "There's nothing to be afraid of, Erin," he murmured. "I won't hurt you this time."

"But-b…it's daylight," she faltered.

"We have to get used to each other sometime," he said reasonably. "And the curtains are drawn. It isn't so much light, is it?"

His hands were behind her, feeling for the clasp of her bra. He found it and loosed it, then gently removed the wisp of lace and silk. His eyes adored her for several long moments before he bent and removed the last silken undergarment. She was a little self-conscious, especially about the scars; but he didn't seem to mind them, and after a minute she relaxed and let him lower her to the bed.

"Get under the covers," he said gently, as if he knew how difficult it was for her. "You don't have to watch me if you don't want to. We've got plenty of time to get used to the sight of each other.''

There were rustling sounds as he undressed, and a minute later she felt him slide under the cool sheets beside her.

''Now,'' he whispered, moving above her so that he could look down into her eyes. ''Now, here, our marriage begins.''

She pushed at his chest until she felt the erotic combination of hard muscle and abrasive hair. Her hands were fascinated by it, by the pulsating feel of it.

He moved the cover down to her waist and looked at her breasts with warm, curious eyes. His hand reached out and touched her there, feeling her go hard, watching her.

Her own eyes followed his, and she saw his long fingers exploring her, discovering the textures, with exquisite tenderness. Her breath caught, because it was new and exciting to realize that he was her husband now, that all the old taboos had been lifted.

''We're married,'' he said as if reading her thoughts. ''Will you try to remember that it's all right for us to do this now?''

''I'll try....'' Her eyes were drawn to his broad, tanned chest. ''You must strip to the waist when you work outside,'' she said curiously.

''I do.''

''I look white compared to you.''

He lifted himself above her, letting his narrow hips move completely over her flat belly, watching her face contract at this new intimacy.

"Now move the cover away," he said, arching over her, "and watch me."

She trembled all over at the soft command, obeying him without even thinking, caught up in a growing tide of erotic pleasure. Her eyes traveled the length of their bodies, to where he was as white as she was; then he moved over her, and she felt the strength of him in an embrace that seemed more intimate than anything they'd done before.

"Oh, Ty…!"

"Put those soft hands on my hips," he whispered, "and hold me to you."

She moaned as his mouth came down over hers, feeling him tense, feeling the weight and warmth and maleness of him settling against her. His tongue probed inside her mouth, and she opened her lips to give him access, feeling him tremble as she moved and lifted toward him.

"You're my woman, Erin," he murmured, his lips a breath away from hers. He caressed her hips, urging them upward, moving them against his. "You're my wife."

She shuddered at the exquisite sensations flowing through her. She reached up, trembling as her breasts brushed against his hard chest, feeling him shudder too, feeling the tide of hunger overwhelm him.

"Sweet," he groaned, nudging her legs apart. "God, you're sweet, you're so sweet, so sweet…!"

His mouth shuddered against hers. He felt her move, heard her moan, and all at once it was happening. His head seemed to explode with the helpless urgency of his body. He moved feverishly against her, over her, feeling her body accept him with only a small spasm of protest.

She clasped his neck with her arms and gasped a little, but before she could begin to feel anything, it was over. He could feel her disappointment and damned himself for his infernal impatience. He was still shuddering helplessly in the aftermath of their lovemaking, but there was no pleasure in it for him now, no satisfaction: Erin had felt nothing.

He lifted his head and looked down at her, seeing the suspicious brightness in her eyes even as she tried to smile.

"Don't do that," he said gruffly. "Don't pretend. Don't you think I know how it was for you? You didn't begin to feel anything; I didn't give you time."

"It's all right—"

"No, it's not all right." He drew in a harsh breath and smoothed the hair away from her flushed face. "Oh, God, honey, I'm sorry," he whispered, bending to her mouth, kissing it with aching tenderness. "I'm sorry. Erin, I don't know how…." He groaned, burying his face in her throat. "I don't know how!"

He lifted himself away from her and got to his feet,

reaching into his discarded shirt for a cigarette. He went to the window and stood staring out the slightly opened curtain, smoking, silent.

She stared at him curiously, uncertain. "Ty?"

"I've only had a handful of women, Erin," he said after a moment. "It was always just sex, nothing more. Just a need I satisfied. But it wasn't necessary to give back the pleasure. So I never learned how. I thought it might come naturally, but I guess it doesn't." He took a long draw from the cigarette. "I guess it doesn't."

She ached for him. With his intense pride, a confession like that must have taken a lot of courage. She got to her feet slowly, favoring her sore hip, and went to him.

"I don't know how to say this," she began, keeping her eyes on his chest. "But I don't think experience is all that important, if two people have a...a mutual need to please each other. I'm glad you haven't cared about those other women, because that makes it special with you. Almost as if I were the first woman for you."

"You are the first woman—in every way that counts," he said.

She lifted her eyes. "Then...then...maybe..."

"Can you tell me?" He searched her eyes. "Or at least show me? I'll do anything you want, anything I can to make you feel pleasure." He touched her hair hesitantly. "I don't get much out of it when I know you aren't enjoying it."

Her lips turned up a little at the corners. "I can't look at you and show you," she confessed shyly.

"You won't have to."

He put out the cigarette and lifted her easily in his arms. "Maybe I can hold back this time, since I'm not so hungry," he said, looking at her with kindling desire. "What do you want me to do?"

She arched her back a little, feeling the magic, feeling her femininity blossoming under his ardent gaze. "You know," she whispered.

"Yes, I think I do." And he bent suddenly and opened his mouth over the peak of her soft breast.

She moaned, stiffening, her voice breaking as she caught the back of his head and held him there.

He tasted her, savored her, as he lowered her to the bed. Her hands guided him, showed him where to touch her, how to please her with his mouth and hands. When he reached the softness of her inner thighs, she shuddered and cried out.

He grew drunk on the sound of those soft little cries, but carefully controlled the pulsating fever of his own body as he tasted and kissed and nibbled at her soft, sweetly scented skin. When he kissed her mouth again at last, she was crying.

He eased over her, slowly this time, and felt her arching under him, felt her hands at the back of his thighs, guiding, showing him where she was the most vulnerable, teaching him the rhythm she needed.

"Sweet," he whispered, opening his eyes to look at her.

She was moaning now, her skin glistening, her hair damp. Her eyes were half closed, glazed, her lips swollen and parted. She gasped and tossed her head restlessly back and forth on the bed. Her eyes opened, wild and frightened, then closed again.

"Shhhh, baby. Shhh." He soothed her with his voice, smoothed back her hair with his hands, comforting her even as he kept up the easy rhythm. "It's all right. Let go for me. Let go. That's it. Don't pull away, don't move back. Lie still and let me have you. Let me have you now."

Suddenly she cried out and opened her eyes wide. Her face contorted, her hands stretched out to the brass bars of the headboard and gripped them until the knuckles whitened. She writhed under him, moaning frenziedly and thrashing this way and that. She began to beg him, whisper to him. Her hips moved with his, moved, moved, until his mind began to feel the pleasure building in his own body.

All at once, her hips ground up against his and held there; she shuddered uncontrollably and began to cry as her body went into spasm after spasm after sweet, hellish spasm.

"Open your eyes!" he groaned, clenching his teeth as it began to explode in him, too.

She did, looking up at him. He saw her eyes for an instant, and then her face blurred as he was hurled through time in an explosion of unbearable brilliance—light and color and rainbows and waterfalls... Then, at last, all was still.

He felt her under him what seemed like hours later, felt her sweaty warmth, her pulsing heartbeat, the tender trembling of her arms and legs, and the faint sound of weeping.

"Oh, God, I didn't hurt you, did I?" He touched her face with his hand, gentling her. "Erin, did I hurt you?"

"No." She kissed his neck, his throat; she clung to him, still trembling softly. "Oh, sweet heaven, I never dared dream...I... Oh, Ty, that was so scary!"

"What was?"

"I...I went wild, didn't I?" she murmured. "I didn't even know what I was saying or doing, I just started shaking and I couldn't stop, and then...then, it burst inside me like an explosion, and I felt as if I were going to die of the pleasure, that I couldn't bear it..."

"The little death." He smiled. "The French call it that. I felt it too, for the first time in my life."

"People could die of it, all right." She clasped her arms tightly around him. "Let me feel all your weight," she whispered. "Lie on me."

He trembled a little at the husky note in her voice.

"Like this?" he asked, giving her his weight. "I might crush you."

"I'd like that." Her hands slid down his muscular body, finding his hips and pressing them down over hers. She began to move, to surge sinuously under him. "Ty, I'm sorry, I can't seem to help it," she whispered.

"It's all right, honey," he whispered back, sliding his hands under her hips. "I'm just as hot as you are. Here." He moved her legs, positioning her, and then he lifted his smoldering eyes to hers and watched as he took her. "Don't close your eyes," he said softly. "This time, I want to see it."

She trembled gently, holding him as he moved. "Again, so soon?"

"I might make the record books," he said wryly, then grimaced at the surge of pleasure. "God!"

She lifted against him. "Can I watch you, too?" she whispered shakily.

"Yes!" His breath was coming wildly now as her body danced with his, matching each sharp move, teaching him, learning from him, in a rhythm that was quick and hard and devastating.

"Ty...Ty!" she moaned.

"Feel it!" he cried. "Feel it. Let me watch you...!"

Her eyes widened, dilated. She shuddered, and then it was all sharp pleasure and vast explosive sweetness, and his eyes were there, seeing her, dilating, bursting

with it. She made a sound, then heard him cry out
even as she saw his face contort and redden, his teeth
clench, his body tense. She felt him in every cell of
her body and clung to him while the world swayed
drunkenly around them....

The ceiling came into sharp focus. She stared at it,
trembling, her skin saturated with warmth and dampness and pleasure. She felt him shuddering over her,
and her hands smoothed down the long, muscular line
of his back.

"We'll kill each other doing this one day," he
whispered.

"I don't care." She nuzzled her cheek against his.
"You're wet all over."

"So are you." He lifted himself away from her and
fell onto his back. "My God. I can't believe I felt
that."

"Neither can I." She sat up slowly and looked at
him, really looked at him, with eyes that revealed
both awe and delight.

He opened his eyes lazily and smiled when he saw
her expression. "No comment?"

She smiled back and shook her head. "How about,
'Wow'?"

He laughed. "I could second that." He stretched
and groaned. "I think we broke my back." Suddenly
he sat up. "For God's sake, your hip!"

"It's all right," she told him gently. "Just a little

sore. The doctor did say I should exercise it.'' She blushed.

''I wonder if that was the kind of exercise he had in mind.'' He grinned. ''Should we discuss it with him?''

She hit him. That, of course, led to a bout of enthusiastic wrestling, which she lost. She laughed up at him, delighting in their newfound intimacy.

''I'll remember next time,'' he said, tracing her eyebrows softly. ''You won't have to show me again.''

She colored more vividly. ''You're incredible,'' she said breathlessly, and dropped her eyes to his chest.

''So are you.'' He bent and brushed her mouth with his. ''And now,'' he said, ''how would you like to go shopping?''

She smiled. ''I guess I can lean on the cane, can't I?'' She laughed. ''I think I'm too weak to walk.''

''Then I'll carry you.'' He lifted her out of bed and set her on her feet. He searched her eyes. ''No more regrets?''

''No more.'' She pillowed her cheek on his warm, damp chest. ''Was this just an impulse, or did you plan it?''

''An impulse,'' he said. ''I couldn't take any more nights like the past several. Cold showers are rough on the system in winter.'' He tilted her chin up. ''And you were pretty jittery. I had a feeling we shared the same problem. Too many hangups, too little privacy. So I thought I'd try it.''

She reached up and bit his lower lip. ''Can I sleep with you from now on?''

He chuckled. ''I think you'd better. The hall's pretty cold at night. And sneaking down it would wear me out.''

''We wouldn't want that,'' she murmured dryly.

''No. We sure wouldn't.'' He tugged her hair. ''Let's get some clothes on. I still have book work to do when we finish in town.''

''Spoilsport.''

He pulled on his jeans, glancing over his shoulder at her. ''The sooner I get done with the books, the sooner we can go to bed.''

She made a grab for her slip. ''Well, what are you piddling around there for?'' she asked. ''Hurry up!''

He laughed softly. For the first time, he had some hope for the future.

Erin, watching him, was entertaining some hope of her own. She felt deliciously weary and fulfilled, and she wondered at his patience and stamina. He had to be the handsomest man alive, she thought dreamily as she watched him dress. He was more man than she'd ever known, and it was all of heaven to be his wife. She smiled to herself. What a beautiful start for a marriage, she thought. It could only get better.

Nine

Erin walked through the stores with Ty in a kind of dazed pleasure. He held her arm possessively, as if he might be afraid of losing her, and she pressed close beside him, drowning in the newness of belonging.

He needed a new watchband, so they stopped in a jewelry store. And after Ty had picked out a band and mumbled something to the jeweler, who was going to put it on for him, the friendly clerk talked him into trying on a huge diamond ring. He put it on and eyed it without much enthusiasm. And Erin got an idea.

She hadn't thought what to get him for Christmas, and she wasn't really sure that he'd like a wedding ring or would even wear one. But she had several hundred dollars saved up. And now she knew that the ring he'd tried on would fit him. He didn't like that one, but she saw him gazing steadily at a gold band inset with a string of diamonds. When the jeweler called him to look at the watchband, Erin motioned to the store clerk, told him what she wanted, and watched him slyly remove the ring from the case and size it. Glancing warily at Ty, he held his forefinger and thumb in a circle shape, and Erin grinned. While Ty was busy she quickly wrote a check and told the clerk to put the ring in a jar of jewelry cleaner.

"What are you doing? I'm ready to go," Ty asked impatiently as the clerk came back with a small sack.

"I needed some jewelry cleaner," she said with a straight face. "I'm ready now. Thank you," she told the clerk.

"My pleasure, ma'am," he replied politely.

"What do you need to clean?" Ty asked. "All you wear is that wedding ring."

"When I can keep up with it." She sighed. "I lost it for a while this morning. I know I left it on the sink, but when I went to get it, it had disappeared. And a few minutes later, it was back." She glanced at his rigid features. "Maybe I'm losing my mind."

"Not likely," he said. "Maybe your eyes were playing tricks on you."

She shrugged. "Maybe."

She didn't see him exchanging a grin with the jeweler. Which was just as well.

He went with her through the clothing stores in the mall, watching curiously as she looked at price tags more than at the dresses and jeans and blouses.

"That isn't necessary, you know," he told her. "You don't have to watch prices anymore. You own half the ranch, for God's sake. I maintain credit in this particular department store. You can have anything you want."

She glanced at him and smiled. She knew he wouldn't begrudge her a dress or two—or three or four, if it came to that. But it was important to her to maintain her independence. And she still didn't feel entitled to any inheritance. She was almost sure that Bruce had involved her mainly to hurt Ty, not because he'd loved her or had wanted to help. She simply couldn't use that money with a clear conscience. And Ty didn't know that she'd just drained her account to buy his Christmas present.

"I don't really see anything I like," she said at last. "I just like window-shopping."

He searched her wide eyes. "Erin, you don't have many clothes...." he began slowly.

"I don't need many, not when I'm just hanging around the house, do I?" she said. "Anyway, I don't care about having a lot of things to wear anymore. The days when I looked good in them are gone."

He looked as if he wanted to say something, then he shrugged and let it go.

The last stop Erin wanted to make was at a Christmas-tree lot. "We have to," she pleaded. "I can't celebrate Christmas without a tree to decorate."

He studied her. "Conchita usually sets up a little manger scene...."

"I want a tree," she moaned.

He sighed loudly. "You'll put yourself in bed with all this walking," he muttered, noticing the way she was leaning on the cane. "It doesn't have to be gotten today, does it?"

"I want a tree," she persisted.

He pulled off the road next to the tree lot and cut the engine, shaking his head. "Women."

"Men," she replied.

He opened the door and got out, and she smiled to herself.

The tree she wanted was a white pine, gloriously shaped and green. It still had its root ball, too, so that it could be planted after the holiday season.

"Oh, for God's sake!" he burst out. "Do you mean I'm going to have to pot the damned thing and then go plant it the day after Christmas?"

"I can't kill a tree in cold blood."

He gaped at her. "You what?"

"I can't kill a tree in cold blood, just to put it in the house for a few days. It isn't natural."

"Neither is this." He glared at the tree and the smiling man who'd just taken his money.

"If you don't let me have this tree, I'll stand one

of your horses in the living room and decorate it," she threatened.

He stared at the tree. He stared at her. He stared at the man.

"Go ahead, say it," she told him. "Come on. Bah, humbug…"

He turned on his heel, grasping the tree in one hand. "Let's go," he muttered.

"You don't have to help me decorate it, either," she said after he'd put it in the trunk, of the Lincoln and helped her into the passenger seat.

"Good."

"You'll get used to it," she said gently.

He glared at her as he started the car and put it in gear. "Don't hold your breath."

She slid over next to him and almost immediately felt his body respond to the nearness of hers. He glanced down and then slipped his arm around her, pulling her even closer.

"That's better." She sighed and pressed her head against his shoulder.

His lips touched her hair, her forehead. His breath quickened. She reached up and touched his face, his rough cheek, his lips. He looked down and almost ran off the road staring into those soft, warm green eyes.

She smiled to herself, savoring his closeness, the spicy smell of his after-shave. In all her life, she thought, she'd never been happier.

They parked in front of the house, but before she

could move away, Ty bent his head and kissed her. It was different from any of the kisses they'd shared before. Softer. More tender. More a caress than a kiss.

"I think we'll put you on the very top," he whispered. "You're as pretty as any angel I've ever seen."

"You sweet old thing," she said, and reached up to kiss him back.

"I'm not that old." He grinned.

She knew what he was thinking, and her cheeks went hot. "Quit that," she said, scrambling out of the car.

"We're married," he reminded her. "It's okay if we sleep together."

"Keep reminding me," she murmured, and glanced up at him. "You make it all sinfully exciting."

He chuckled. "So do you, wildcat."

"I'm going to get a bucket for the tree," she said, turning.

"Let Red do it," he replied. "You get off that leg before you break it. You've done enough walking for one day."

"Yes, Your Highness," she muttered.

"What are you going to decorate it with?" he asked suddenly.

She grimaced. "I forgot. Well, maybe Conchita can think of something."

"Maybe," he said.

The minute she went inside, he found Red, told him what he wanted done with the tree and slipped him a twenty-dollar bill to go and buy decorations.

Red gaped up at his boss. "Buy what?"

"Decorations," Ty said shortly. "For the Christmas tree."

"Christmas tree?"

"You eat a parrot for breakfast or something?" Ty demanded. "She wants a tree. She wants it decorated. I got the tree, but I don't have any decorations. There's twenty dollars." Ty nodded toward the bill. "Go get her something to put on it!"

Red whistled and pulled his hat low over his eyes. "Talk about earthquakes."

"I'll quake your earth if you don't get going."

"Yes, sir."

He walked off, shaking his head and muttering.

Ty glared after him. "You'd think he'd never seen a damned Christmas tree," he mumbled to himself as he headed for the house.

"The *señor* is putting up a tree? Inside the house?"

"A Christmas tree," Erin told Conchita. "To decorate."

There was a long, breathless garble of Spanish. "Never before." She shook her head. "Never, never. No tree, no fuss, he say; never mind turkey and things. Christmas is only for other people. Now here he buys a tree. I tell you, this is not the same man for whom I work since he is a young man. This is a stranger, *señora*. He smiles, he laughs, he compliments me on breakfast...." She threw up her hands. "A miracle!"

She went off to tell José about it, leaving Erin standing, amused and ummoving, in the hall.

"I thought I told you to sit down," Ty said, tossing his hat onto the side table.

"Well, I—Ty!"

He jerked her off her feet cane and all, and carried her into the living room, where a fire crackled merrily in the hearth. "Can't have you hurting that hip, can I?" he murmured. "I have plans for it later."

"Oh, do you?" she said, smiling as he found her mouth and kissed it gently.

He dropped into an armchair next to the fireplace and wrapped her up against him.

"Conchita told me you don't usually have a Christmas tree," she said lazily as his lips brushed hers.

"We don't. Not since my father died. It depressed me."

"Did he like Christmas?" she asked, fascinated.

He leaned back against the armchair, letting her head fall naturally onto his shoulder. "Sure," he said, smiling at the memories. "He was like a big kid. I bought him an electric train set the year before he died, and he played with it by the hour. He told me once that they'd been so poor when he was a kid, all he'd ever gotten in his stocking was fruit and nuts. He'd never even had a store-bought toy.''

"Poor old soul," she said gently. "Did they love him, at least?"

"I don't think they'd wanted him," he said. "They had to get married because he was on the way. They never forgave him for forcing them to the altar."

She studied his collar, thinking about the child she'd lost. Some of the brightness went out of her.

He traced her cheek. "Don't look back," he said as if he knew what she was thinking. "We can't change the past."

She sighed. "I guess not."

He studied her averted face. "I sent Red after some decorations for the tree."

"Oh, Ty! That was nice of you," she said, diverted.

"I just thought it would be a shame to stand a live tree up in the house with nothing on it," he said. "People would stare."

"That's true." She cuddled closer. "Do you suppose we could forget my exercises tonight?"

He shifted her on his lap. "No," he said with a smile, and kissed her.

"Tyson!" she muttered. "I've walked around half the day!"

"That's good, but it's not what the doctor ordered. You want to walk again, don't you? Properly, I mean?"

"Yes," she admitted, then grimaced. "All right. I'll do the horrible things."

"That's my girl."

The odd thing was that she felt like his girl. There was a tenderness between them now that she noticed in the simplest acts. At dinner that evening, he seated her at the table. He creamed her coffee. And when he wasn't doing things for her, he watched her, stared at her with the most curious expression. She felt protected and safer than ever before in her life.

"Did your mother even come to see about you?" he asked as they sat over a second cup of coffee.

She shook her head. "She and I have never been close, you know."

"Why didn't Bruce tell me about the wreck?" he wanted to know, his eyes narrow and piercing.

She hesitated. It was just one more thing that would hurt him, and she'd had enough of that.

"Why didn't he?" he persisted.

"Ty, he wasn't deliberately cruel," she said, choosing her words carefully. She touched the back of his hand where it rested beside his coffee cup. "He was possessive...just obsessed with me—I wish I'd realized it sooner, but I didn't. Maybe he was afraid to tell you; or just didn't think you'd care..."

His face closed up. He turned his hand over and touched her fingers lightly. "He knew I cared," he said. "After he told me that bull about your opinion of me as a lover, I stayed drunk for two days. José told him about that.''

''Oh, Ty,'' she breathed.

''I got over it.'' He looked up, his face harder than ever. ''But I hated you for a while. If he'd told me about the wreck then...'' He searched her wide green eyes, the elfin face in its frame of lustrous black hair, and the anger seemed to drain out of him. ''Oh, hell, I'd have been there like a shot, who am I kidding?'' he muttered. ''I'd have walked straight through hell to get to you if I'd known you'd been hurt and needed someone.''

Yes, he would have, she thought. But he didn't add that he would have done the same for any hurt or sick person. She knew how generous he was when people were down on their luck. Conchita had told her things about him—things she'd never known before—about the good works he did anonymously.

Her hand closed around his. ''They told me that I was calling for you when they brought me in. It was already too late to save the baby, but I felt so empty and alone and frightened,'' she recalled, studying his lean hand. She saw it contract jerkily around her fingers.

He stood up suddenly, moving away from the table. ''I'd better get that paperwork done,'' he said in a harsh, haunted tone.

She could have bitten her tongue for what she'd said. It just put up more walls between them. He was

retreating into his, right now; withdrawing from the
pain of the past.

"Ty…" she began.

"You'd better decorate your damned tree," he said
without looking at her. "You can do those exercises
later."

She threw down her napkin and stood up. "I wasn't
trying to get at you," she said desperately. "You take
every single thing I say at face value."

He turned and looked at her, his eyes blazing. "Do
I? And without reason? You haven't forgiven me for
what happened. In your heart, you blame me for the
condition you're in and for losing the baby. And
maybe I blame myself, too. Bruce made mischief, but
I believed him. So did you. Maybe neither of us is
willing to go that last step—to trusting each other. I
haven't had any more practice at trust than you have.
So it might not be a bad idea to step back and take a
look at things before we start making commitments
we don't really feel."

Her mind was spinning. She'd never heard him
make such a long speech, and she didn't understand
what he was saying. Did he mean that he didn't want
a commitment to her? Did he want her to get well so
that she could go away and leave him?

She started to ask him, but he was already striding
away, lighting another infernal cigarette. She stared
after him blankly for a moment, then got slowly to
her feet and dragged herself into the living room. All

the buoyancy, the magic of the day, seemed to have vanished.

It was hard going, standing long enough to get the decorations on. Conchita helped her dress the magnificent tree, talking animatedly about other Christmases when the *grande señor* was still alive, about all the company they'd entertained and the lavish parties they'd given.

"Never any parties since then." Conchita sighed. "Señor Ty does not like people."

"Especially female people," Erin muttered darkly, glaring at the ornament in her hand.

"*Sí*, that is true," Conchita agreed, taking the phrase at face value. "It is because of his looks, I think. He is sensitive about them, and he thinks no woman could ever care for him because he is not, how you say, a magazine pinup." She smiled and shook her dark head. "How sad, because it is not how a man looks, but what he is, that attracts a woman. Señor Ty is *muy macho*—you know, like my José. He will always be the man in the house, and that is how it should be."

Erin could have said something about that, but she bit her lip. She was in enough trouble with him already.

Ty didn't say a word about her tree when he walked into the living room later that evening. She was in her leotard, working out; he sat and watched her and coached for a few minutes, but his heart wasn't really in it.

"Do I get to sleep with you tonight, or am I still in the doghouse?" she asked finally, brushing back her damp hair.

He just stared at her, as if he couldn't quite believe what he'd heard. In fact, he didn't. He'd been sure she wouldn't let him near her, and here she was making propositions. He pondered over it until he decided that women probably felt the same urges men did, especially when they'd had a taste of fulfillment. She could therefore want him physically without loving him. Which was a bitter realization, because he'd only just come to the conclusion that the physical part of it wasn't all he wanted anymore. Somewhere along the way, he'd awakened to other needs: emotional ones.

"Do you want to sleep with me?" he asked, searching her eyes. "Now that you've had a taste of it, you can't live without it; is that what you're saying?"

It was like a slap in the face. She didn't see his hurt pride or his own insecurity or the disappointment he felt at what he interpreted as a self-centered expression of physical need. She only heard cutting words that made her feel like a tramp.

"I guess I can just turn on the electric blanket instead," she said after a minute, her eyes averted. "I can live without sex, thanks."

He started to speak, closed his mouth, got up and stomped out of the room. Erin stared after him with tears in her eyes. She couldn't bear the change in him, and all because she'd been trying to tell him that she loved him. She did love him, she realized. Perhaps she always had. At first, it had been a challenge to catch his eye, to make him notice her. And then, at some point—she couldn't say when—it had become something deeper, stronger. During all those long months of physical torment and mental anguish, the thought of him had sustained her. She'd wanted him so badly then; had wanted to call him, to tell him. But Bruce had managed to convince her that Ty despised her, that he still wanted nothing to do with her, especially now that she was a cripple. So she'd withdrawn into her shell and told herself she hated Ty for causing what had happened to her. But she hadn't, not really. One look at him was enough to open her heart, and being around him, with him, near him, had reawakened all the old hungers. Yes, she loved him. But in trying to tell him so, nervously working up to it, she'd only alienated him. And now there didn't seem to be a chance in the world of healing the old wounds.

As the days passed, things went from bad to worse. Ty ignored her. Unfortunately, his men weren't so fortunate; his temper was hot enough to start fires, and even Conchita and José were beginning to feel the heat. The food wasn't seasoned enough, the coffee wasn't strong enough, his car wasn't being cleaned properly, the stairs had dust on them. Everything irritated him. And when he wasn't complaining, he was locked in his study with the books. He hadn't touched Erin since they'd gone into San Antonio. He didn't seem to want to anymore, and she felt neglected and unwelcome.

By Christmas week, Erin began to notice how much she'd changed since coming to Staghorn. She'd been doing her exercises faithfully, even though Ty no longer watched her, and she was making some progress. She could walk for the first time without the cane. Her scars were fading. Her face had regained most of its radiance, and she was gaining weight. She looked more and more like the model Bruce had first brought to Staghorn—and the prettier she got, the angrier Ty got.

He'd begun to see her the way she'd been: a beauty, a lovely fairy who could have had any man she wanted, any time. And then he looked at himself in the mirror and knew that he didn't have a hope in hell of holding her. Once she was completely well, she'd leave, go back to the old life, and he'd be alone. Well, damn it, he told himself, he'd known that from the beginning, hadn't he? He'd set out to shock her back to life and get her on her feet again; to make up to her for what he'd cost her.

She was well on the road to recovery. But he couldn't bear to get too close to her. His heart was vulnerable. If he didn't watch out, she'd carry it off to New York with her. It shocked him, disturbed him, to realize how vulnerable he was. He didn't want to care about her. He wanted to be whole and independent. But she was sapping him. He'd seen himself that day in San Antonio—so drunk on her that he was like a pet instead of a man, fawning on her. He'd hated his weakness. He kept hearing his father tell him not to let any woman do that to him; to keep himself strong, in command. All his life he'd denied those hungers, and now they were bringing him to his knees.

Finally, one morning, he decided it was time to fight back, to confront Erin—and himself. He headed for the living room, where he knew she'd be doing her exercises, then stood in the doorway for a moment, watching her with narrowed eyes.

When Erin saw him, she got to her feet with a minimum of awkwardness and brushed back her hair. "Yes?" she asked politely. "Did you want something?" She felt as if she were talking to a stranger. He was unapproachable now, carefully girded in his emotional armor. The iron man all over again.

He lifted the smoking cigarette in his hand to his lips, staring at her with amused contempt, the way he'd looked at her in the early days. It embarrassed her.

"Not bad," he said. "You're getting your figure back."

"Don't make fun of me," she said, keeping her voice even as she shifted from one foot to the other. "I can't help the way I look."

"That makes two of us."

She perched on the arm of the overstuffed chair and looked at him. He was thinner and, there were new lines in his face. Suddenly she realized how little communication there had been between them recently.

"Something's wrong, isn't it?" she asked, startling him. "And not just between the two of us."

He drew on the cigarette and blew out a thin cloud of smoke. "Guessing?"

She shook her head. "You look worried."

"I'm having a few financial problems," he said after a moment. "Or should I say, *we're* having a few financial problems, Mrs. Wade?"

"How bad is it?" she asked.

"Bad enough." He sighed. "I invested heavily in a consignment of grain to feed my cattle this winter. The silos were owned by a corporation that defaulted, and the grain was confiscated. That set me back on feed so I had to take a loss by selling off cattle in a bad market. One investment balances another, you see," he explained. "One loss causes another. Kind of like dominoes. We may pull out, we may not. It's going to take some quick thinking and a lot of legal advice. At that, we may lose half of what we own."

She smiled gently. "Well, half isn't so bad, is it, considering the size of Staghorn?"

"Could you live with half a body?"

"I've been doing it, haven't I?"

And that's all it took to set him off again. Without another word, he wheeled and walked out of the room. She cursed under her breath. If just once he'd stand still and talk about things!

She couldn't remember ever having had such a miserable Christmas. She'd wrapped his present and put it in a huge box, wrapped that, and put it under the tree. And all the time, she worried about what he would think. Their marriage was in terrible shape, yet she'd bought him a very expensive wedding band. She'd thought about returning it, but her stubborn heart wouldn't let her. As long as there was a ghost of a chance that he might someday learn to care for her, she couldn't give up. And maybe he'd like the diamonds, even if he didn't like the symbolism of the ring. Besides, he could always hock it if he got desperate for money, she thought, and then was astonished at her own cynicism.

She was up and dressed early on Christmas morning. Ty was already sitting in the living room when she walked in, and he looked wonderful in tailored slacks and a neat striped shirt. His hair was clean and meticulously combed, his face shaven. Erin knew he'd done it for her sake, and she wanted to thank him—or at least smile at him—but there'd been too much tension between them lately; she felt awkward and uncomfortable just being around him.

"Merry Christmas," she said politely.

"Merry Christmas." Ty stood up as she approached, motioning her to sit down across from him. He noticed that she was walking without her cane, and without limping noticeably. The emerald-green dress she had on complemented her eyes, as did the soft, natural-looking makeup she had artfully applied. Her hair was brushed forward, curling softly and framing her elfin face. All in all, she looked refined and thoroughly lovely. "Very nice," he murmured. At her expression of surprise, he added hastily, "The tree, I mean."

Erin glanced at it, then looked underneath and was faintly surprised to see a gaily wrapped package beside those she already knew were for José and Conchita.

"You got me something, didn't you?" he asked shortly, glaring at her.

"Well, yes…"

"So I got you something."

It was a big box. Of course his was, too, but that was just camouflage. She wondered if he might have done the same thing, then shook her head. Too wild a coincidence, she told herself. She poured some coffee from the elegant silver service Conchita had set up, then selected a sweet roll and settled back in the overstuffed armchair.

"You're walking much better these days," he observed. He leaned back against the sofa with his coffee cup in hand.

"I've been working hard," she replied.

"Quite a change from those first few days here."

She moved her shoulders restlessly. "Yes. Quite a change."

He sipped his coffee quietly. "Want to give out the presents?"

"Okay." She got up, faltering a little as she knelt. She heard him behind her, calling to José and Conchita.

They came in, grinning, took their presents and gave small ones to Ty and Erin. Then everyone opened their gift boxes and exclaimed over the contents. Erin found a beautiful shawl that Conchita had hand-crocheted for her and Ty, a muffler. Conchita opened a set of handkerchiefs from Ty and a small silver box from Erin, and José got a tie and a wallet.

"Muchas gracias." Conchita grinned. "Now is okay if we go over to my sister's house, just for a little while, until time to serve the dinner?"

"Sure," Ty told her. "Go ahead."

"We come back soon." She laughed. "Thank you for these," she added, clutching her presents, and José echoed her thanks. Then they left, closing the door behind them. And Erin and Ty were alone, completely alone, for the first time since the day they'd bought the tree.

Ten

Erin finished her coffee nervously, wishing that she and Ty could go back to the early days of her residence here and recapture the budding magic of being 9ogether. There seemed to be such an insurmountable barrier between them now. He was always on the defensive—perhaps out of his own guilt—and she couldn't reach him anymore.

He seemed to be nervous himself, if his chain-smoking was any indication of it. He moved restlessly to the tree, picked up her present and handed it to her.

"We might as well get this out of the way," he said gruffly, pausing to pick up the box with his own name on it.

Erin, sitting quietly with her present beside her on the sofa, felt really uncomfortable as she watched him open it. What was he going to think of the ring? Would he be angry? Would he be surprised?

He removed the wrapping and looked inside at the smaller box. Glancing curiously at her, he picked it up, slowly unwrapped it and then opened it.

His expression was one of numb shock, and Erin wanted to go through the floor.

She got up and knelt a little awkwardly beside him. "I'm sorry," she said, reaching for the box. "It was a stupid thing to do. I didn't mean—"

He caught her wrist. "Here," he said in an odd, gruff tone. "Put it on."

It took a moment for her to realize that he wanted her to put it on his finger. She fumbled it out of the box nervously and slid it onto his ring finger, relieved to find that it was a perfect fit.

He looked up then, his eyes strange and glittering, holding hers.

"You don't...mind?" she faltered.

He put his hands on either side of her face, searching her fascinated eyes, and bent over her. His mouth descended, pressing her lips softly apart, shocking her with the aching tenderness of his kiss.

Tears stung her eyes as she closed them. It had been so long since he'd touched her, since he'd kissed her. She caught her breath as he deliberately deepened the kiss, tilting her face at a sharper angle to give himself better access to her soft mouth.

She wanted to reach up, to hold him to her and savor the sweetness of being near him at last. But it was too soon; there had been so many misunderstandings between them, so much grief. She couldn't be sure he wasn't just trying to find some new way to torment her.

She pulled back gently and lowered her face.

He sensed her withdrawal, and the tenderness he was feeling for her clouded over with pain. She was building a wall of her own now, and thanks to his black temper, he wasn't going to get past it easily.

"Thank you," he said. He wanted to add that he wouldn't take the ring off until he died, that it would always remind him of her.

"You're welcome," she said shyly. "I...bought it the day we went to San Antonio."

He remembered that day all too well; it had haunted him ever since. His face went hard with bitter regret. "What did you buy it with?" he asked suddenly. "You wouldn't let me stake you."

She shifted a little, tugging at the skirt of her dress. "I...had a little money saved."

He looked down at the ring. Diamonds. Real ones, set in gold. "My God," he said under his breath. His eyes met hers and saw the embarrassment there. "This was expensive."

She only looked more uncomfortable.

He sighed as he looked at the box he had wrapped for her. It was nowhere near as expensive as her gift to him. He hadn't known how she'd feel about a ring now, so he'd taken back the ring he'd bought her before all the difficulties began and traded it for an emerald necklace—a very small emerald, with a few tiny diamonds, on a slender gold chain. It had reminded him of her—bright and delicate and beautiful.

"I wish I'd taken more trouble over yours," he said hesitantly.

"I'll like it," she assured him.

He handed her the package and she opened it, finding that he had indeed duplicated her camouflage. She opened the first box, then the second, and caught her breath at the sight of the exquisitely crafted necklace nestled in the velvet lining of the box.

"Oh, it's so lovely," she whispered, touching it. "It's the loveliest thing I've ever seen!"

She took it out gently, fingering it, her face bright with pleasure, and he forgave himself for not having gotten her something more expensive. She seemed to be genuinely pleased with it.

She laced it around her neck and secured it, lovingly touching the stone as she smiled. "Thank you," she said softly, her voice tender and husky, her face so beautiful that he wanted to take her in his arms and lower her to the carpet in a fever of passion.

Her eyes caught the flash of desire in his, and she hesitated about touching him. But in the end, her pleasure at his gift forced her forward. Shyly, she reached up and kissed the corner of his mouth, just faintly brushing it.

"Thank you so much, Ty," she whispered.

He stiffened at the touch of her lips, trying not to betray how vulnerable he felt when she came close. Her gentle rejection of him earlier had hurt. He didn't want to risk it a second time, so he didn't touch her. When her lips moved away, he just looked at her, noticing the heavy shadows under her green eyes, the paleness of her face. She was beautiful, but there was a haunting sadness about her, a sadness he felt responsible for. He felt responsible for a lot of things. His conscience had disturbed him for days, for weeks. She might forgive him someday, but he couldn't forgive himself. And his growing feeling for her had only made it worse, had only deepened his guilt. He'd struck out at her in pain, but she couldn't know that. And he was too proud to tell her.

"I'm glad you like it," he said, rising. He moved away from her, pacing restlessly.

"The financial situation," she said after a minute. "Is it any better?"

His broad shoulders lifted and fell as he felt for a cigarette and lit it. "Not appreciably."

She bit her lower lip, thinking. She was walking much better now. And the more she exercised, the better she got. Before long, she'd be walking easily. The facial scars were fading, too. She was a new woman already. And she had talent, and the contacts to go back into modeling. Perhaps she could make enough money to help him out.

She sat back down on the sofa. "I've been thinking," she said hesitantly, glancing at him. "I'm improving every day. In a little while, I might be well enough to go back to New York and get back on with my agency."

His back went ramrod stiff. So here it was—she was feeling her beauty again. She was missing the old life, and she wanted to leave. She was hungry for—how had she put it?—the bright lights and the excitement. And maybe for a man whose face didn't look like the side of a cliff. He laughed bitterly to himself. At least he had no illusions about her feelings for him. He hadn't fooled himself into thinking that just because she responded to him physically, she felt anything emotionally.

"If that's what you want, go ahead," he said carelessly. "It might be a good idea, after all."

She'd known he was going to say that. Even so, his saying it gave her a sinking feeling, and she struggled to speak normally. "I can't go immediately, of course. I'll need a little more time."

"Wait until spring, if you like." He sounded indifferent, but the silvery eyes she couldn't see were telling a different story.

"No, I won't need that long," she said quickly. "I'll just take another few weeks."

"Suit yourself." He took a long draw from his cigarette and studied the ring she'd put on his finger. He loved the feel of it, the symbolism of it. When she'd bought it, she must have felt something tender for him, at least. The memory of it would have to last him all his life, through all the years without her, without his love.

He thought about the child she'd lost, and his eyes darkened with pain. She'd felt alone, she said, and empty. And he remembered that, and ached to think of her with no one to look after her, to care for her. She'd been all by herself in that hospital, and he wondered...

He turned unexpectedly and saw her watching him. "You wanted to die, didn't you?" he asked gruffly.

She blinked. "What?"

"After the accident." He held the forgotten cigarette carelessly in one lean hand. "You wanted to die."

How had he known that? She hated discussing it. Every time they talked about it, he got worse, more distant, more unapproachable.

"I thought my life was over," she said slowly. "I suppose, for just a little while, I didn't care about living."

He examined her carefully, noticing the becoming weight gain, the silkiness of her hair, the brightness of her eyes. "I guess you damned me to hell every time you thought about me," he murmured.

"I wanted to call you," she confessed, flushing.

He didn't move. He didn't breathe. "You...what?"

"I wanted to call you. I almost did." She searched his narrow eyes quietly. "But Bruce convinced me that you had no use for me, that you wouldn't have spoken to me anyway," she said. Her eyes darkened with remembered pain.

"I would have come, though," he said.

She tried to smile. "I think I realized that before, but it was nice to hear it, all the same. It feels so terrible now. I hated you for all the wrong reasons, for things that Bruce was responsible for. But I believed him, you see."

"I guess you had enough reason not to question what Bruce told you," he replied, his voice deep. "I'd been unspeakably cruel to you."

She searched his face. He had such a poor opinion of himself; how could she tell him that she thought he was the sexiest man alive, and that she grew as shy as a schoolgirl every time she was near him?

"Why?" she asked gently. "Was it really just because you wanted me?"

"What other reason could there have been?" he countered brusquely, drawing away.

Once, she thought wistfully. Just once to shake him out of his brooding, to unsettle him. She wondered what he'd do if she peeled open her bodice and let him look at her.

He walked to the door, touched the doorknob and

hesitated. "I've got a new colt in the barn," he said with his back to her. "Want to come look at him?"

The invitation was unexpected, and it thrilled her. She smiled shyly. "I'd like that, yes."

"You'll need a jacket. It's cold out today."

She followed him into the hall, forcing herself to take slow, easy steps and not to limp. She was proud of her progress, and it showed in the radiance of her elfin face, her big green eyes. She laughed as he held out a denim jacket to her. It was broad and long-sleeved and had to be one of his.

"That will swallow me," she protested.

"You don't seem to have a winter coat," he replied, hesitating uncharacteristically. "I couldn't find one in the closet a few days ago."

She smiled at him. "I used to have a full-length mink. I sold it, after the...after I... Oh, Ty, don't," she said, the smile fading at the look in his eyes. "Please don't. You said yourself that it was in the past, and it was. We can't go back."

"I wish we could," he said fervently. "I'd give anything to change it."

"Here," she said as she handed him the coat. "Put this enormous thing on for me, and I'll try not to trip over the hem."

He actually laughed, although it was quick and faint. "All right. Put your arms in."

It was cold outside, and a little misty, and the sky

was as gray as Ty's eyes. He took her arm, propelling her toward the large, modern barn.

All his hands had the day off, and most of them were away from the ranch with near and distant kin, celebrating Christmas. Erin followed Ty into the cool interior and waited until he closed the door. Then she followed him down the long, neat corridor that separated rows of clean, straw-filled stalls, only a few of which were occupied.

"Don't you have many horses?" she asked curiously.

"We," he corrected "have quite a few. But we only bring the expectant mamas in here."

"Because of the cold?"

"That's it." He stopped at the next stall and turned her to the right. "There he is. Born last night."

He was an Arabian. Pure black, with the small head that denoted a purebred stallion, and so tiny. He walked on spindly legs that seemed too tiny to support him, and his proud mama licked and nuzzled him. As she watched, Erin marveled at the ability of an animal to show such tenderness.

"Most mares make good mothers," he said, smiling at the little one. "You won't know him in about a month, when he's got the freedom of the paddock and can toss his head and gallop. He'll be a different colt then."

She leaned back against the side of the stall, searching his dark face. "You love your animals, don't you?" she asked.

"It's easy to love animals," he replied, pinning her with his eyes. "They can't hurt you, except maybe physically if you abuse them or pen them in a corner."

"And people can."

"I learned that as a boy," he told her. "Anything different gets attacked, haven't you figured that out by now?"

"Were you so different?" she asked.

"Big feet, big ears, a face only a mother could have loved, and a black temper," he replied. "You tell me."

"I did notice the black temper," she murmured.

"When?" He laughed coldly. "You haven't come near me lately."

"How could I, when you've avoided me?" she replied, her eyes kindling. "You've done everything except ask me to leave."

"I can't do that," he said. "You're half owner. And my wife."

"In name only."

"Not since that day in San Antonio," he replied curtly, and the memory was in his eyes, like a fire burning.

"That's right," she agreed, deliberately misunderstanding him. "Not since. Not once." She let the denim jacket slide down her arms, oblivious to the shock in his eyes. Her hands went to the bodice of her dress and began to unfasten the buttons.

"What in hell are you doing?" he demanded. But his eyes were watching her hands, not her face.

"I've gained weight," she said. "I thought you might like to see for yourself."

Without questioning her own motives, her own hunger, she opened the last button and slowly peeled the dress down her arms. The material was medium-weight, so she hadn't bothered with a bra. Her breasts were high and full and firm, and she displayed them brazenly, her heart throbbing wildly in her chest.

"Erin…"

She liked the rapt expression, the appreciation that darkened and narrowed his eyes and quickened his breathing. She came close to him, quietly removing his coat while he watched her, disbelieving. Slowly she unbuttoned his shirt, exposing his broad, hair-matted chest to her exploring hands. She smiled in satisfaction as the thick, cushy hair tickled her palms.

"Oh, Ty…" She slid her arms under his shirt and around his waist, so that she could press her taut breasts against him.

"God," he groaned. He caught her shoulder and moved her abrasively against him so that he could feel her silky firm flesh and aroused peaks brushing against his muscular chest. She was so warm, so sweet.

His heart ran wild when her hands found him, blatantly caressed him in a place she'd never touched before. He almost went to his knees with the force of the passion she aroused.

She felt his hunger for her and moved closer, letting her thighs touch his, drowning in the remembered pleasure of flesh against burning flesh.

"Your skin is hot," he whispered roughly.

"So is yours." She arched backward so that she could see his face. Her own was flushed with hunger, her eyes fiercely passionate, her lips parted sensually. "I want you."

"Yes, I know," he said, his voice harsh and almost unrecognizable. "I want you just as much."

Her breath sounded ragged as it sighed out. "Here," she whispered. "Can…we?"

"I think we'll have to," he replied with bitter humor, shuddering a little with his own arousal. He bent and lifted her, pressing his mouth hungrily against one full, perfect breast and glorying in her passionate response.

She moaned sharply, opening her eyes as he lifted his head. She shuddered in his hard embrace, feeling his body absorb the shock of his steps as he carried her to the end stall, which was filled with clean hay.

"No one will come, will they?" she asked.

"No one will see us, or hear us." With one hand he jerked a clean piece of canvas off the wall to use as a cover over the soft but prickly hay. Then he lowered her to their makeshift bed and slowly peeled the dress down her hips, taking her lacy undergarments and hose with it in an undressing that was pure seduction. His lips followed the movement of his hands, and he used them both to drive her wild, nibbling hungrily at her soft hips, caressing her thighs slowly, rhythmically, until he felt her arch and shudder helplessly beneath him.

He touched her then, and she cried out, because it had been so long, and it was so sweet. His warm hands on her body made her forget the chill of the stable and the sting of the cold cloth against her back. She lifted toward those exquisite hands, begging for them, savoring the exquisite roughness of them on her soft flesh. He felt himself throbbing all over with pleasure as he gazed into her lazy, misty eyes and saw her need for him.

"Oh…" she moaned, hurting for him, so on fire with the pleasure he was giving her that she couldn't quite hold it all. She bit her lip, trying to keep quiet.

"Cry out if you feel it like that," he whispered, his voice rough with passion. "Let me hear you."

"I…ache," she whimpered, trembling as he rubbed tenderly at the sensitive peaks of her breasts.

"Not half as much as I'm going to make you ache now." He bit at her soft lips, teased them, rubbed at them, laughing sensuously when she reached up and caught his head and dragged his mouth down hard onto hers.

The kiss they shared was hotter and wilder than

anything that had come before. She couldn't get enough of him. She was drowning, and only he could save her.

"Please, now," she heard herself whisper into his demanding mouth. "Please, Ty, please, please…"

"Shh," he whispered gently. "Shh. Just a minute. Just another minute."

He moved a little away and removed his clothing slowly, watching her, feeling her eyes on him. He had a good body at least—if not a good face—and he liked the way she looked at him with those lazy, hungry green eyes. She shifted on the cloth, her hips moving sinuously, her eyes promising heaven.

He eased down beside her, and she touched his hips, pulling, half pleading.

"Not yet." He touched her softly, watching her arch and moan. "Not just yet. I want to make you beg me this time," he whispered roughly. "I want to watch you cry."

"Please…!"

His mouth covered hers and his hands touched her in new, unfamiliar ways, and for minutes that stretched like exquisite torture, he taught her new ways to ache. She lost her ability to reason in the throes of the most unbearable pleasure she'd ever experienced.

Finally he eased her down onto the cloth and moved over her, his hands on her thighs, his chest crushing gently over her taut breasts. He looked at her as she opened her tormented eyes and breathed in helpless shudders, her nails digging into his flat hips in fierce pleading.

"Easy, now," he whispered, his own voice unsteady, husky with controlled passion. He moved a little and felt her jerk, and saw her eyes dilate frantically. "Easy," he persisted, watching her eyes as he overwhelmed her in a slow, tender rhythm that had the effect of dynamite on her overstretched nerves.

She began to cry at the exquisite tenderness, the slowness of his movements as he deepened his thrusts and his weight gradually began to settle over her. She felt abrasive hair, warm, hard muscle and the heavy, quick throb of his heart over hers.

He slid his hands under her head, gently cradling it, and then saw her face contorting. "Don't close your eyes, sweetheart," he whispered tenderly. "Let me look at you. That's it. Lift up. Lift. Lift... Feel the rhythm. Feel it with me. Lift up... God, Erin, you...make me whole...you make me...sweet... you're so...sweet... God, Erin, God!"

He arched above her, shuddering, shuddering, and she felt it and felt it; a gentle kind of anguish that was terrible in its sweet, slow intensity, like giant hands crushing her with a throbbing warmth that consumed everything in a maelstrom of sensation.

He was whispering something, and she was crying, sobbing, her arms clasped furiously around him, her body trembling softly under his.

She felt his hands smoothing her hair; soothing, comforting her. He kissed away her tears with tender lips that searched over her face in an agony of caring. "Sweet," he breathed shakily. "Like a tender avalanche, flinging me up into the sun, burning me alive!"

"I didn't know it could be like that," she whimpered, clinging closer, feeling him in every cell of her body as he lay over her. She bit him, bit his shoulder, his neck, with bites that were gentle and possessive.

"It can be again." He moved softly against her. "It can be...now."

She shuddered a little, moving with him. Her face curved into his throat this time, savoring the throb of his body against her own as he slowly increased the sweet rhythm.

His mouth slid over hers while they loved. When it happened the second time, it was like a crescendo of fireworks, tender and slow and long-drawn-out, so that she vibrated like a taut bowstring for a long, long time until she felt the echoing vibration of his strong male body over hers; until she heard him moan her name in sweet anguish, and shudder and finally collapse gently on her damp body.

His mouth moved warmly on hers. "If you hadn't taken precautions," he whispered unsteadily, "we'd have made a baby just then."

She clung closer, her eyes closed. "I know," she said softly. "Oh, Ty, we never loved like that...!"

"It was loving, wasn't it?" he murmured. "Because that wasn't sex. There was nothing lustful about it, about what we did together." His strong body shuddered. "Erin, I'm on fire for you."

"And I am, for you." She closed her eyes tightly and clung to him. "Ty, why are you punishing us both for what happened? Why can't I sleep with you? Why can't we have a real marriage?"

He nuzzled his face in the hollow of her warm shoulder. "Is that what you want?" he asked. "A real marriage? I thought you wanted your career back."

She bit her lip. Was this a good time to tell him what she really felt: that she never wanted to leave him? That more than anything she wanted to have his children and grow old with him?

She swallowed. "Ty...I could stop taking the pill," she said hesitantly. Her arms contracted as she felt him go rigid. "We could make another baby."

He almost stopped breathing. Was that what she really wanted? Was it guilt, or pity for him, or was she addicted to making love with him? Could she settle for him, when she might have her career back? He wanted to take what she was offering. He wanted it desperately. But he owed her a chance at the old life, to make sure that it didn't have an unbreakable hold on her. She had been crippled and hurt, and she had bitter memories. Would he be taking advantage of a momentary weakness—one she'd regret when she was completely well?

He lifted his dark head and looked into her questioning eyes. "Not yet," he said gently. "Not right now. We'll sleep together, if that's what you want. God knows, it's what I want; I walk around bent over because I need you so desperately. But no babies. And no commitments," he added. "First, you go back to New York for a few weeks and pick up the threads of your old life. Then, when you've had a good taste of it and I've got my financial mess straightened out, we'll make decisions."

She searched his eyes. Was that an offer or a hedge? Did he really want his freedom? Was it all only pity? If only she could read him. Even in passion, he held back.

"All right," she said after a minute. If this was all she could expect, perhaps it would be enough. He wanted her, and that could grow into something lasting.

She'd go back to New York. Then she'd come home and show him that his looks didn't matter to her, that she could see any number of handsome, sophisticated city men and still prefer him. She smiled slowly. She'd get him; she already had a hold on him—he just hadn't realized it yet. She felt new, whole, hopeful. Her face radiated with beauty.

"Look at you." he chided, letting his eyes slide down her body. "In the middle of winter..."

"Look at you, tall man." She smiled up at him.

"You seduced me," he accused softly, smiling

back. "Taking off your dress, baring those pretty breasts... I couldn't have stopped to save my life."

"You stopped long enough to torment me out of my mind." She blushed with the memory of how she'd begged for his body.

He bent and nipped her lower lip tenderly. "You begged me. You can't imagine what that did for my ego, hearing you plead with me to take you. God, it was sweet!"

"My poor, battered pride..."

"You loved it, you little liar," he murmured gruffly, burning her mouth with his. "You laughed up at me while I was having you...!"

She moaned as his mouth opened to explore hers in a kiss that was as intimate as lovemaking, sweet and heady and hungry.

Suddenly he pressed his face into her throat and groaned. "I want to," he whispered, "but I can't; I'm so damned tired!"

She smiled against his hair. "I'm tired, too." She sighed, gloriously content, and closed her eyes. "Can I sleep in your arms tonight?"

A fine tremor went through the hands holding her. "My God, of course you can!"

She sighed again, relaxing, feeling the warm hardness of his body against hers. "I don't want to get up."

"I don't either. But we could have visitors in here, and I don't think we'd ever get over the embarrassment," he murmured, smiling. He dragged himself away from her and sat up, studying her lovely, relaxed body. "So beautiful," he said absently, tracing her hips, her long legs. "I could look at you forever and never get enough."

She smiled. "You're not bad yourself."

"That's the way I feel right now," he confessed, and laughed with pure pride. He tossed her dress and underthings to her. "Better get those on while I can still drag my eyes away."

"Flatterer," she said demurely while she struggled to get dressed, feeling the cold for the first time and shivering a little.

He was dressed before she was, so he helped her button up between kisses, then lifted her to her feet.

"Why the canvas?" she asked curiously, pulling straw out of her disheveled hair.

He reached down and picked up some hay, showing her the briars liberally mixed in with pieces of straw. "Hay isn't just hay," he mused. "It's briars and wild roses and weeds and such. Think about how that would feel on your bare back with my weight over you."

She blushed scarlet at his words, and he smiled almost affectionately and bent to brush a tender kiss against her forehead.

"I love watching you blush," he murmured. "I love knowing there's been no one except me."

She nuzzled her forehead against his warm mouth.

"I like knowing that you haven't been to bed with half the women in the county, if we're making confessions," she replied. "I could have gone down on my knees when you told me that day in San Antonio that you'd never really made love before. It was heaven."

"Some women wouldn't have thought so."

She pulled back and looked up at him. "I'm your wife," she said gently.

His chest swelled with pride as he looked at her. "Yes," he said. "My wife. My woman."

She pressed warmly against him, savoring his strength and the new affection between them. If only it would last this time, she thought, closing her eyes on a prayer. If only it would last! She had him now.

Oh, Lord, she prayed silently, *please, please let me keep him this time. Let him love me. Just let him love me, and I'll have everything in the world that I'll ever need or want.*

Eleven

There was still a part of Ty that Erin couldn't reach. They made wonderful, satisfying love together, and at night she slept in his hard arms. But the closeness came only in bed; the rest of the time he was the cold, taciturn man she'd first known. He watched her, frowning, as if he were worried. She exercised and grew strong, and eventually the day came when she had to go to New York—not because she wanted to go, but because Ty still insisted she prove to herself that she was whole enough to work again. And she didn't dare wonder if he wasn't just tired of having her around, if the guilt had worn off at last.

He drove her to the airport, and she had to fight

tears every step of the way. He carried her suitcase into the terminal and waited for her to check in. Then he escorted her to the concourse, waiting while she selected her seat.

After she'd finished, she turned to him, her eyes dark green, troubled. He didn't allow himself to read things into that look. She felt sorry for him, he decided. She was going back to the life she loved, and because he'd made that possible by shaking her out of her apathy, she felt grateful to him as well. But he didn't want pity or gratitude, or even the magic of her body burning against his in the darkness. He wanted her love. Just that.

She came close to him, realizing belatedly that ever since the morning in the barn, when she'd tempted him, she'd had to make all the moves physically. He'd lie beside her in bed at night and never touch her unless she showed him that she wanted him to. It was an odd kind of relationship. He gave her anything she asked for, from dresses and trinkets to lovemaking, but only if she asked for it.

"Will you miss me, at least?" she asked with a faint smile.

He returned her smile. "The bed will get pretty cold," he observed.

"I'll mail you a hot water bottle," she assured him.

He touched her cheek gently, searching her face. "If you ever need me, all you have to do is call. I'll be on the next plane."

She smiled at the possessive note in his voice. He did feel protective of her—there was no doubt on that score. "I'll remember," she promised. Then they were calling her flight, and she looked up at him fearfully, gnawing on her lip.

"It'll be all right," he said gently. "You're strong now. You'll do fine."

"Will I, really?" she asked, trying not to cry. She searched his eyes. "Kiss me goodbye, Ty," she whispered.

He bent his head, holding her by the shoulders, and brushed his lips softly against hers. "Be a good girl," he whispered.

"What else could I be, without you around?" She laughed brokenly. "Oh, Ty...!"

She threw her arms around his neck and dragged his mouth down over hers, oblivious to other passengers, to passersby. She held him and savored the warm, hard crush of his hungry mouth, and drifted and drifted and drifted...

He pulled back abruptly, his eyes flashing, his face taut with desire, and she had to catch her breath and her balance before she moved away.

"Call me when you check into the hotel," he said tersely. "I want to make sure you got there all right."

"I will." She looked at him one last time, already feeling alone. "Take care of yourself."

"You, too."

She couldn't say goodbye. The word was painful,

even in thought. She forced a smile and turned toward the tunnel that led to the jet. She didn't look back.

It was a short but trying flight. She cried most of the way there. Her leg was better; she was walking comfortably these days. She felt and looked at the peak of health. But her heart was hurting. She wanted Ty. And now he seemed not to want her anymore.

When she got to the hotel and into a suite that he'd insisted she book, she called him. But it was a brief conversation. He seemed to be in a blazing rush—took just long enough to remind her to call if she needed him, and then excused himself and hung up.

She stared at the receiver, feeling dismissed. Deserted. She cried herself to sleep. The next morning she felt stronger, and furious at him for not rushing up to bring her back home, to tell her he couldn't live without her. Then she laughed at her own stupidity. Ty would never do that; he needed no one.

She went by her old agency and talked to the man who'd represented her before. He was amazed at how well and strong and recovered she looked, and he arranged immediately to have a new portfolio shot. A week later, she was working.

Days passed with dull regularity. The life she'd once found exciting and fascinating was now little more than drudgery to her. She kept thinking about the ranch and Ty. She missed the sound of cattle in the meadows. She missed the leisurely pace and the quiet of the country. She missed Conchita's merry prattle and the fresh flowers that had graced the tables each day. But most of all, she missed the feel of Ty's hard body in the darkness, the warmth of him when she cuddled close and felt his arm go around her, his chest firm and comforting under her cheek. She missed watching him around the ranch, hearing the deep, measured sound of his voice with its faint drawl, the sound of his boots as he came in to supper every night. She missed the rare smiles and rough hunger in his voice when he made love to her. She even missed those homely, uneven features. She wondered what he'd think if she wrote and told him that she thought he was the handsomest man alive? He'd probably burn the letter, thinking she was being sarcastic.

She drove herself relentlessly, working long hours every day until she was weary enough to sleep at night. Every few days she called home, but Ty always seemed to be in a hurry. He never talked, except to exchange comments about work and the weather. He didn't ask when she was coming back. He didn't even ask if she was coming back. He didn't seem to care one way or the other.

That was when she began to worry. Perhaps he'd decided that life was sweeter when he could be alone and not have to put up with a wife he didn't really want. Perhaps he felt that guilt and pity alone could not sustain a marriage. She began to brood over it, and once, right in the middle of a photographic session, tears stung her eyes at the thought of living without Ty. The photographer stopped shooting and sent out for coffee and a sweet roll, thinking she was hungry. She was—but not for food.

In the end, she stood it for a few weeks—until spring was just beginning to melt the snows and brighten the skies; until Ty's very indifference shook her from wounded pride to fury.

She took the first plane home one day, right after she'd finished a commercial; she looked and felt viciously angry. Enough, she told herself. She'd had enough of his practised indifference. If he wanted a divorce, she'd give him one, but he was going to have to come right out and say he did. She wasn't going to be ignored to death. And even while she was thinking it, something inside her was dying. She loved him more every day. The thought of doing without him for the rest of her life was killing her.

It had all begun the wrong way, for all the wrong reasons. But she no longer blamed him for her troubles. In a way, she blamed herself. She needn't have believed Bruce's lies. She could have gone to Ty with them from the very beginning and avoided all of it. And she could have made him listen that day, instead of meekly accepting his bad temper—which had probably been nothing more than wounded pride, because he'd believed Bruce, too. If she'd made him listen, perhaps he'd have taken her in his arms and asked her to marry him, and they'd have had their baby....

She shook herself. That was over. She couldn't change it. So now she had to go on— With him or without him. But she knew that going on without him would be a kind of death—a life without pleasure or warmth or love. There could never be another man; she loved him too much.

There was no one to meet her at the airport, because no one knew she was coming back. She rented a car and made the long drive to Ravine without stopping. She went straight through town and out to Staghorn, where she pulled up in front of the house, glancing around. Well, the Lincoln was there. He could be out, of course; he had roundup in early spring. But she had a feeling he was somewhere nearby.

She got out of the car and looked from the house to the corral. A number of the men were gathered around the corral, calling enthusiastically to somebody on a horse.

With glittering green eyes, she walked down to them. She knew instinctively who it was on that unbroken horse. And sure enough, when she got there, she saw her tall, lean husband giving the animal a run for its money. He was wearing denims, wide leather chaps, and the old worn Stetson that looked near retirement age. His face was animated, full of challenge and male pride, and the animal was tiring. It leaped

and bucked while the cowhands yelled encourage-
ment to the tall, relentless rider. Finally, the weary
horse gave up and trotted around the corral, panting
and sweat-lathered.

Ty swung gracefully out of the saddle, patting the
animal gently before he handed it over to one of the
men to groom and water. Erin watched him with her
hands in the pockets of her skirt; it had been all too
long since she'd seen him, and her eyes devoured him
hungrily. He was so much a man. A Texan.

He turned unexpectedly and saw her, and froze in
place. Before he had time to say anything, she lifted
her chin pugnaciously.

"Well?" she asked, glaring at him. "You might at
least say hello, even if I'm not welcome. And while
we're on the subject, thanks for all the cards and letters and phone calls; I sure enjoyed them!"

He climbed over the corral fence and dropped
gracefully to his feet to approach her, while behind
him the men stared and punched each other—they
loved a good fight.

"Welcome home, Mrs. Wade," Ty said with faint
mockery, but his eyes were running over her like
tender hands. It had been a long time, and she was
beautiful, and he wanted her until it was a raging
fever. But she was different, too: eye-catching and
expensive-looking in a pretty red-and-white outfit.
The long white sweater overlapped a full red crinkle-
cloth skirt that swirled around her calves when

she walked, and she'd belted it with a macramé tie. Her hair was longer now, over her shoulders, softly waving, and her face was exquisitely made up. She was the perfect model. His eyes narrowed as he wondered how many men had looked at her and wanted her. Had she wanted any of them? He could only imagine how he'd compare with those city men. His face went hard thinking about it. He was going to lose her—so what the hell; he might as well help her leave, convince her that she didn't need to feel sorry for him anymore. The guilt was mostly gone. He had a few twinges now and then, but he could live with himself now. He didn't need her pity.

"Hello, yourself," Erin replied curtly. He sure didn't look like a man who couldn't sleep at night for missing her.

"Did you come back to get your gear?" he asked, pausing long enough to light a cigarette.

"Maybe I did." She straightened. "I can see how welcome I am."

"What did you expect, a brass band?" he asked. "I got along my whole life without anybody in the house. It's pretty pleasant, if you want to know."

"Well, New York isn't bad, either," she retorted, stung. "I'm having a glorious time! I work every day, in fact, and I'm much in demand for parties and such."

"Found somebody else, have you?" he asked with

apparent indifference. "I hope he's rich. You'll be expensive to keep."

"As if I ever cost you a dime, Tyson Radley Wade!" she shot back, raising her voice.

"Radley?" Red Davis drawled from the corral fence.

Ty whirled, silver eyes blazing. "Stuff it, Davis!" he growled.

Red saluted him, but he shut up all the same.

"That's it, yell at the poor man," Erin said scathingly. "Nobody around here is allowed an opinion except you!"

"You don't have to start yelling out secrets, do you?" Ty asked, scowling.

"Oh, was your middle name a secret?" she asked innocently, and looked past him at the cowboys. "Well, it's not anymore."

"Why don't you go pack your damned bag?"

She stomped her foot. "Can't wait to get rid of me, can you? Why did you bother to marry me in the first place?"

"Because I didn't want Ward Jessup digging holes in my pasture looking for oil!" he said coldly. "That was it, that was all of it. That, and a little pity. You sure as hell were a basket case when I found you!"

"And now, thanks to you, I have a wonderful future in store!" she replied angrily. "I love living alone! I have the time of my life walking around stages while middle-aged hippopotamus women try to imagine themselves in dresses that would barely fit around one of their legs! I love being ogled by male designers and hurried by dressers and pestered to death by photographers and harassed by perfectionist directors on commercials! It's great coming home to an empty apartment and spending my whole weekend watching roller derbies and championship wrestling!''

The cowboys were trying not to laugh. Ty was gaping at her. He'd never seen her like this.

She clenched her small hands at her sides, her elfin face red, her eyes sparkling dangerously. ''I hate you, you big ugly cowboy!'' she raged at him. ''I'm tired of waiting for the phone to ring and haunting the mailbox for letters that never come! They've offered me a week in Saint-Tropez to shoot a swimsuit commercial, and I'm taking it! The director is French and tall and handsome and sexy, and he wants me, and I'm going!''

''Like hell you're going!'' he burst out, throwing down the cigarette with a violent flick of his wrist. ''You're not traipsing off to the south of France with any damned Frenchman!''

''Why not?'' she demanded, her voice high-pitched. ''You don't want me! I'm just a burden to you, just a cripple you're carrying around on your conscience!''

''Some cripple,'' he murmured, studying her.

''I wish I had a wooden leg, I'd kick you with it, you arrogant cattleman!''

He smiled slowly.

"My, my, aren't we wound up, though?"

"'Wound up'?" She backed away a step, eyes narrowing. "Wound up! I'll show you wound up...."

She picked up the nearest object—an empty bucket sitting by the fence—and hurled it at him. He ducked, so she grabbed a bridle off the corral and threw that, following it with a piece of loose wood.

The cowboys were chuckling behind Ty. He glared at them as he dodged the wood.

"Ship me off to the city, will you?" She pushed back a strand of sweaty hair, looking around for another missile. "Throw me out on my ear, give me over to the mercy of strangers. A fine way to treat your own wife!"

"You never wanted to be my wife," he said. "You married me to get even with me!"

"Sure I did!" she cried, grasping a horse collar. "To get even with you for ignoring me all the time, for baiting me, for killing me with your indifference. You big, stupid man, I love you so much!" Her voice broke as she flung the collar. "I've loved you from the first day I saw you, and you've given me nothing but hell!"

He didn't duck. The horse collar was heavy and it caught him in the chest, but he didn't even flinch. His eyes were wide and unblinking as he gaped at her, disbelieving. Had he heard right?

"It was never Bruce I wanted!" she practically

screamed at him. "It was you! You, with your homely face and your big ears and your big feet and your mean temper! I cared so much…and you didn't even like me! I tried so hard to make you care, but you hated me!"

He'd heard right. And at that realization, something inside him burst and bubbled up like a spring. She was still raging, something about hating him because he was dumber than a cactus plant, but he didn't even hear her—he just started to walk toward her like someone in a trance.

She loved him. Yes, it was in her eyes, in her face, in everything about her. She'd reached a peak now, her voice broken and wounded, and she was going to leave him and go be a famous model….

In midtorrent, he bent and lifted her in his hard arms and put his mouth over hers. He wasn't rough. He couldn't have been rough with her—not now. But he wasn't that gentle, either, because it had been so long and his mouth was hungry for the sweet softness of hers.

She mumbled something for a few seconds before her mouth opened and her arms crept around his neck, and he tasted tears on her lips as she kissed him back.

The cowboys were grinning and chuckling, but neither of them heard. He turned, walking with her in his arms toward the house, opening his eyes only to keep from tripping as he went up the steps and through the front door.

"Señora!" Conchita laughed as she opened the study door for Ty. "Welcome home."

"Umm-hmm," Erin murmured under the crush of Ty's mouth, waving languorously as he walked through the door and kicked it shut behind him with one booted foot. He started walking again, then suddenly wheeled and locked the door.

She felt the sofa cradle her back and the weight of Ty's body settle completely over her. Her eyes opened a little as his mouth lifted just long enough for her to take a breath.

"Ty..." she whispered.

"Are you blind and deaf and dumb?" he asked, his voice deep and harsh. "Look." He held up the hand that was wearing the ring she'd given him. "Does that tell you anything, little shrew, or do you want the words? I'll give them to you, but once I start saying them, I may not be able to stop."

She touched his mouth, feeling its rough warmth. "I wouldn't mind," she whispered, her eyes loving, exquisitely tender.

His hands cupped her face. "I love you, Erin," he said fiercely, looking intently into her eyes. "I loved you the day you left here, and I was hurting until I thought I'd die of it. I didn't realize it...and I listened to my ego instead of my heart and ran you away. Oh, God, I've loved you so much, and not ever believed that you could love me back. I've been cruel, because I was so damned afraid of losing you...!"

"Losing me," she repeated ironically. "As if you could. I adore you. I love all the nooks and crannies of this face." She touched his lean cheeks while his eyes closed and he shuddered and thanked God for the fact that love was blind. "I love all of you, with all of me. And there is no man on the face of this earth who is handsomer or sexier or more tender than you are. Oh, you sweet big dumb man, you," she said lovingly, drawing him down to her. "I'll love you until I die. Until you die. And forever afterward."

He crushed her up against him, burying his face in her throat, shuddering with the fulfillment of every dream he'd ever had. "Erin," he whispered.

The unashamed adoration in his tone made her tingle all over. She bit his ear gently and cupped his face in her hands, making him look at her.

"Ty," she said softly, searching his eyes, "I'm not taking the Pill."

"Aren't you?" he asked unsteadily. His hands found her macramé belt and loosened it. Then they eased the hem of the sweater up over the lacy little bra she was wearing.

"You could make me pregnant if we…" She hesitated, feeling oddly shy with him.

"What a hell of a turn-on," he whispered, biting tenderly at her lips. He lifted his head and looked right into her eyes. "Say it."

Her lips parted, trembling, because she knew what he wanted her to say. It was the right time, at last—

for the healing balm for all the wounds they'd inflicted, for the ultimate expression of the love they felt for each other.

"Give me a baby, Ty," she whispered with aching tenderness. "This time, let's make it happen."

He searched her eyes for a long moment, then slowly bent his head. And it was a kind of tender loving that erased every other time, that healed all the wounds, opened all the doors. He held nothing back, and neither did she. And what they shared was so profound, so exquisitely sweet and fulfilling, that she cried for a long time when it was over—tears of pure ecstasy—lying in the arms of the man she loved most in all the world.

She looked up at his face, adoring it, pushing back his damp black hair with hands that trembled.

"I love you," he whispered.

"If I hadn't known already," she replied, "I'd know now. We never loved like that. Not even that day in the stall when you made me cry."

"I wasn't sure of you then," he said gently. "I wanted to see if I could make you tell me what you felt. But I couldn't."

"You couldn't read my mind," she murmured. "Inside, I was screaming it."

"So was I." He bent to her mouth and smiled as he kissed it. "Come home, Erin," he breathed. "I'm lonely."

"I'm lonely, too." She nuzzled her face against his

chest and smiled again. "But I never will be again, and neither will you. I'll never leave you."

He didn't say anything. He didn't need to. His mouth brushed down upon hers, and the fires began to burn again. She reached up her arms and closed her eyes and kissed him back.

Epilogue

Ed Johnson checked his briefcase one last time before he knocked on the door at Staghorn. Conchita let him in, grinning from ear to ear.

"You look like the cat left all alone with the canary bird," he said. "What's going on?"

"*Señor*, you will have to see it to believe it," she assured him. "Such changes in this house in the past year! I am constantly amazed. Come. I will show you."

She led him to the doorway of the den, and he stopped there, staring. Tyson Wade was lying on his back on the carpet with a fat, laughing baby sitting on his flat stomach, and Ty was laughing with it.

He turned his head sideways as Ed entered the room. "Good morning."

As he spoke, a second baby crawled up from his other side and pulled at his hair, cooing.

"You're baby-sitting the twins?" Ed asked.

"Erin's upstairs," Ty told him. "But I change a mean diaper. Got the papers?"

"Right here," the attorney said, patting the briefcase. "You made a hell of an amazing recovery, you know. Last year about this time, you'd just escaped bankruptcy."

"I had a strong incentive." He grinned. "A pregnant wife can sure light a fire under a man. And twins put wood on it."

"How old are they now?" Ed asked, kneeling beside Ty to grasp a pudgy little hand and be cooed at.

"Just five months," Ty replied. "We sit and stare at them sometimes, trying to believe it."

Ed remembered the baby Erin had lost and smiled at the tiny miracles. "Twin blessings," he murmured.

"Thank God." Ty looked up at the older man and laughed. "If you'll hold up that contract, I'll try to sign it."

"No need," Erin said, smiling as she joined them. "I'll take the boys while you do the honors."

"There's just one thing," Ty told the attorney as Erin scooped up Jason and Matthew. "If Ward Jessup blows a gusher under just one of my cows…"

"He won't. And he promised to lease just what he

needed. Amazing,'' he murmured, watching Ty
scrawl his signature on the contract, ''how the two of
you finally sat down and ironed out your differences.
That feud's been going on since you were barely out
of your teens.''

''Not so amazing,'' Ty said, glancing past his attorney at Erin, who was cuddling the babies on her
lap and looking so beautiful that his breath caught.
''No, not so amazing at all.''

Ed followed his rapt gaze and smiled. Ty had
changed, and so had his outlook. He wondered if Erin
knew how great a difference she'd made in the taciturn rancher's life, just with her presence.

She looked up at that moment and met his curious
gaze. And she grinned. Yes, he thought; she knew,
all right.

He packed up the contracts and said his goodbyes.
As he walked out the door, he looked back and saw
Erin handing Ty one of the boys with a look of such
love that he turned away, feeling as if he were tres-
passing. Outside, the air was sweet with the smells of
summer. He drank in a deep breath of Texas air.
Maybe there was something to that marriage business,
he decided. He'd have to start looking around. Babies
were pretty cute, and he wasn't getting any younger.

He got into his car. The windows were down, and
just as he started the engine, he heard the sound of
deep, vibrant laughter coming from the open windows
of the house. Ed smiled to himself and drove down

the winding driveway. Out by the fence, the prickly pear cacti were in full bloom. Sometimes, he thought, the ugliest plants put out the most beautiful flowers. He guessed there was a man back the road a piece who wouldn't argue with that statement one bit. And neither would the woman who'd put the bloom there.

* * * * *

▼ SILHOUETTE

❯ SPECIAL EDITION ❮

COMING NEXT MONTH

THE NINE-MONTH MARRIAGE Christine Rimmer

Conveniently Yours

When a night of passion left Abby Heller pregnant, Cash Bravo vowed
to marry Abby and give the baby his name...then he'd let her go to find
herself a younger mate. But Abby has only ever wanted Cash...so she's
not about to let *him* go!

THE RANCHER MEETS HIS MATCH Patricia McLinn

Dax Randall is known locally as 'Mr Impossible'. Resistant to the
advances of any eligible young lady, he has to swallow his pride when
his teenage son needs a lesson in love. Visitor Hannah Chalmers *seems*
a safe date...but she's soon dangerously close to stealing his heart!

WILDCATTER'S KID Penny Richards

Switched at Birth

When Russ Campbell left her pregnant six years ago, Laura Ramirez
vowed to put him out of her mind—and heart—completely. Now he's
back in town, and is about to discover the son he never knew he had.
But would this only be a temporary reunion—or could it be forever?

TEXAN'S BRIDE Gail Link

When bachelor tycoon Clay Buchanan decides it's time to settle down
and raise a family, love is the last of his priorities. The perfect solution
is a marriage of convenience to his assistant Linda Douglas. But Linda
has a secret—she loves Clay and intends to be a *very* devoted wife!

THE MAVERICK MARRIAGE Cathy Gillen Thacker

Hasty Weddings

When Susannah divorced Trace McKendrick, she carried with her a
secret. Seventeen years later, Trace and Susannah have two days to re-
wed to meet the terms of eccentric Uncle Max's will. But simple
maths proves to Trace that Susannah's eldest son is also his!

BABY ON HIS DOORSTEP Diana Whitney

That's My Baby!

Executive Colby Sinclair has his life mapped out to the minute, until
his sister leaves her baby on his doorstep. Help arrives in the shape of
beautiful, off-beat neighbour Dani McCullough. Could *she* be a part of
the ready-made family he never knew he wanted?

CHRISTIANE HEGGAN

SUSPICION

Kate Logan's gut instincts told her that neither of her
clients was guilty of murder, and homicide detective
Mitch Calhoon wanted to help her prove it. What neither suspected was how dangerous the truth would be.

*"Christiane Heggan delivers a tale that will leave you
breathless."*

—Literary Times

1-55166-305-8
**AVAILABLE IN PAPERBACK
FROM SEPTEMBER, 1998**

JASMINE CRESSWELL

THE DAUGHTER

Maggie Slade's been on the run for seven years now.
Seven years of living without a life or a future because
she's a woman with a past. And then she meets Sean
McLeod. Maggie has two choices. She can either run,
or learn to trust again and prove her innocence.

"Romantic suspense at its finest."

—Affaire de Coeur

1-55166-425-9
AVAILABLE IN PAPERBACK
FROM SEPTEMBER, 1998

EMILIE RICHARDS

THE WAY BACK HOME

⤷⤶ ★ ⤷⤶

As a teenager, Anna Fitzgerald fled an impossible situation, only to discover that life on the streets was worse. But she had survived. Now, as a woman, she lived with the constant threat that the secrets of her past would eventually destroy her new life.

1-55166-399-6
AVAILABLE IN PAPERBACK
FROM SEPTEMBER, 1998